They arrived at th
overlooking the ocea ,
swell was peaking beneath a moderate
offshore breeze.

The walls of glass they had dreamed about
and waited for had appeared, and were
beginning to peel off left and right out near
the rocks. The sun was low in the
early evening sky.

DANIEL TRIBE
began surfing in the early days.
After living in France, Portugal and Spain
for some years, he moved to Morocco where
he stayed for a further three years before
travelling extensively around Scandinavia,
Thailand and North America.

is his first novel.

DANIEL
TRIBE

full MOON RED *sun*

EverGreen Graphics

CRAIGWEIL ON SEA
ALDWICK

full
MOON
RED
sun

First published in the United Kingdom 1999 by
EverGreen Graphics

ISBN 1 900192 02 0

Design and production by Cecil Smith
Typeset in 10/14 Cheltenham by
EverGreen Graphics
11 the Drive, Craigweil On Sea, Aldwick,
West Sussex PO21 4DU

Printed and bound in the United Kingdom by
RPM Reprographics (Chichester) Ltd
2-3 Spur Road, Quarry Lane,
Chichester, West Sussex PO19 2PR

Contents

The
Seance

*T*HE SURF was clean and bright. There was no more scraping the frost off their boards, shivering in wet suits. They pushed out through the white water to ride the big waves that loomed like grey walls of glass before they shattered on the rocks. It was Spring. The gentle offshore breeze had sculptured the waves to perfection.

Mike watched the tanned legs of his best friend's girl probe the waters edge as he began paddling out. The swell was running at six to eight feet, with clean sets and good lulls, so getting out to the line up was quick and easy. He just made it up the face of an eight foot peak as his friend Steve took off on it.

The sun was rising, and as the lip of the wave began to curl it was lit orange and gold by the early morning rays. From the top of the section Steve took a slow diagonal down along the face and then up again. He trimmed his board, moved his weight towards the front, and crouching low he dipped his head against the blue green belly of the beast as it curled over him.

Then suddenly, it turned from green to a mass of white foam as the wall collapsed. He was knocked from his board and dragged down over the falls.

It was 1969, north Cornwall, the days before leg ropes, and losing a board usually meant a long swim. Mike was lucky. When he finally surfaced his board was close by, he swam to it and turned turtle, hanging in the water as the next three of four waves crashed over him. In the lull he paddled back out to his friend, waiting for the next set.

'Saw you wipe out. Cool!'

'Yeah, well, if this wind holds up I reckon we could make some of those sections!'

'That would be great wouldn't it?!'

The wind did hold up, and for two hours or more they took wave after wave until they had to come in, exhausted.

As Spring turned to Summer the swells came less frequently, but when they came the offshore breezes came with them. The early morning was best. The water was clear and warm, on calm days they used to go out for long swims, and hang out on the beach until sunset. If there was a swell in the evening they slept out under the stars and got into the water early as the sun came up.

✳

Then Summer became Autumn and the nights got cold, too cold to camp out. They rented a cottage, sharing with a guy they had met sitting watching the sun set as they came out of the surf one day. They began to hang out with him, fascinated by his tales of Turkey and India where he said he had been living for years. He was short, with a mop of thick black hair brushed across his forehead, dark brown eyes and a strong black moustache. His name was Paul. Mike and Steve were tall and blonde, hair bleached by the sun and the surf. Together they were a strange lot, made stranger by Paul's sidekick, 'One Hand Ian', who had a withered hand he kept in a black glove, close to his chest inside his jacket.

In the cottage, as the nights drew in, Paul used to tell stories about his life in India, he gave everything a sense of magic, that in everything around them something else was hidden.

Winter finally closed its grip and the surf was nearly always blown out. Mike and Steve took jobs. Steve worked with the first person making surf boards in England.

'It's only because you're American.' said Mike. Mike got a job as a swimming instructor at the local pool.

'It's only because you've got a sun tan!'

If the surf was up they went out, but the water was cold as an iron fist.

One night they sat round lazily, half expecting Paul to begin one of his stories, but he suggested having a seance.

Steve and Mike swapped looks, both thinking it was odd.

'Why?' asked Mike.

'Why not?' said Paul, 'you write down letters of the alphabet on separate bits of paper. We can use this table here.' He pointed to an old round table in the middle of the room.

The cottage had no electricity, but they had some candles, and in their light they sat in the cottage listening to the rain, waiting for Paul to direct things.

'I'll put this in the middle, put your fingers on it – make sure you don't put any pressure on the rim.' he said.

In the distance they could hear the surf crashing onto the beach. A log cracked on the fire, and Paul kept his eyes on them, black in the flickering light.

The glass began to move slowly, as if it had a life of its own. Mike raised his finger a fraction from the rim, to make sure he was not putting pressure there, he guessed Steve would do the same. The glass began to dart around the alphabet. Paul said matter of factly they had 'made contact', and must find out more. He began to ask the spirit its name, whether it was friendly, and whether he could help it. It spelt out the following, which he wrote down. 'Spirit's name, Axlethe. Friendly. Unhappy. Cannot help.'

Paul asked if it minded them being there, whether it had any messages for them. It spelt out; 'Do not mind, do not drive yellow car, going now.'

Paul tried to 're-contact' the spirit but the glass never moved again.

'You may as well put that stuff away', he said, with a

nod of the head in the direction of the table and pieces of paper. 'Burn them'. They threw the letters on to the embers of the fire, and watched them turn yellow and black before disappearing.

A week later Paul went up to London to meet 'a friend'. The surfers had never met any of Paul's 'friends', apart from One Hand Ian. It seemed that he was keeping them separate, as if he was grooming them for something later on. Anyway, they were almost relieved when he didn't come back. January became February and suddenly early March. They stopped working, and began to go up to the coast when the surf was up. For days on end they would paddle out near the rocks where the waves peeled off left and right on the road to God; silver and purple, green and gold, backlit by the yellow haze of the sun, the waves broke into a million jewels they thought they would keep forever.

Steve used to drive up to the coast in an old yellow Austin Healey. He had had a bike accident in the States before leaving, and blew the whole of the insurance monies on the car.

'I used to see an old guy back in the States with one of these, but I could never afford one. When I came here it was the first thing I fell in love with!' He looked sideways at his girlfriend, Jay. 'Then I met Jay, it's been perfect ever since!'

'Asshole!' said Mike.

'What do you wanna go and leave a beautiful place like California for to come here?' the Brits would ask.

'Well, the weather of course! And I met this Aussie, who told me about all the brilliant waves here and how you could always get any wave you want 'cause the Brits are such crap surfers!'

'I'll see you up there then!'said Mike.

'If I don't get there first!' Steve stuck his board long-ways by the passenger seat of the old yellow Healey. He turned the key and the car's glowing metal ignited, firing on all six as his girlfriend climbed into the black leather seat between his board and the gear shift. She kissed him and they waved goodbye to Mike, shouting 'see you outside!' as they drove off. A thrush's song cracked the air, and the last drops of rain hung onto the oaks around the cottage.

The road up to the coast was familiar to Steve and he drove in a classical way. On either side was forest, oak and beech mainly, fresh and green in the early morning. Rabbits sat motionless on the verge, noses twitching.

In his stone cottage Matthew Treggiar was sipping his first mug of tea that morning; the geese had been making a row outside, his wife was in the bathroom and his little boy was quiet. He put down his mug and headed towards the duck pond shouting the boy's name 'Jack!' He came out of the wood shed smiling. 'I thought there might have been a fox in there, because the geese were making all that noise! But there's nothing there, just stupid old woodlice and things!'

'Well, maybe there'll be one tomorrow son' said Matthew 'come on, it's time for school, let's get going,

I'm taking you this morning!'

He took the boy's hand and led him through the narrow back door of the cottage. As they went in, the phone rang; it was the farmer, his boss, asking Matthew to go down to the main house and have a look at his wife's car which wouldn't start. Matthew cursed to himself, shouted up the stairs to his son to get a move on, and went out to warm up his old Landrover.

Steve switched on the radio and dreamed of hi-fi on wheels; Neil Young's voice took his mind back to northern California and home. A lot of his friends were receiving draft papers for the war in Vietnam which had been steadily escalating. Like a lot of them, he could not see why America had such a presence there. His father was a World War Two and Korean veteran, and had grown cynical about the administration at home.

'It all ended the day they shot JFK', his dad said, 'This government's sold us out.'

'What if I get my draft papers, what do you think I should do?' Steve had asked him.

'It's up to you son, it's your decision. In the last war we knew who we were fighting and why, and it was the same in Korea. This war's different.'

'Why?'

'Money, son. The military's the country's biggest customer and we need the military and the military needs wars. Hell, it don't matter to us if those Vietnamese people want Ho Chi Minh, we won't even let them have an election because we know sure as hell Ho Chi Minh's going to win it! What kind of support of democracy is that?!'

'Yeah, but aren't the North Vietnamese supported by the Russians and the Chinese?'

'No.'

'So what shall I do then?'

'Well, you're always on about seeing the world. You don't have any draft papers, you can go to college here if you wanted and then may be still get drafted, or you could take a bit of time out. Go to Europe.' His father smiled, his blue eyes shining with the unspoken love of the father for his son. 'Hell, you got that insurance money now for that metal you got put in your leg, you could be in London in twelve hours!'

Three days later he was.

He put his hand on Jay's thigh and looked at her for a second, she smiled back, beautiful as ever.

Matthew Treggiar had forgotten his plug spanner. The HT leads in his boss's car were damp and he had dried them out; he had cleaned the rotar arm, checked the battery connections, the coil and starter motor; fuel was pumping through, and there was nothing left but to have the plugs out, clean them and re-check the gap. If that didn't work he would have to start again.

It was 9 a.m.; he felt the pressure of time emanating from the main house, from the 'any progress Matthew?' and the mannered but definite pacing on the gravel drive by his boss's wife.

'Another ten or fifteen minutes should do it' he said, 'I just need to whip out the plugs, won't take a minute, I need a plug spanner, I'll pop back to the cottage and get it.'

He jumped in to the Landrover, praying that the spanner was where he had last seen it, by the old vice his father had left him, on the oak bench in his workshop. He knew his son Jack had been using it to fix his bike's imaginary ills, and hoped he had put it back.

The Landrover bounced and jolted over the track in two wheel drive, Matthew was keeping the momentum of the diesel engine by pressing his right foot hard down. As he approached a small junction where the track crossed the road, he kept going, and by the time he saw the yellow Healey, it was too late.

Steve tried to miss the Landrover as it pulled straight out in front of him, he went for the trees by the roadside. He bounced off one into another which threw the car onto its side, it travelled a few yards and slammed up against an oak. Both passengers were thrown clear, and lay still on the ground.

2

The Trip

MATTHEW ran to the girl. Her face was heavily cut and bruised, and one leg was obviously broken. She was conscious, her eyes flickered, straining to focus.

'You'll be alright, I'm getting help,' Matthew blurted. 'I'm just gonna check your friend.'

Steve was starting to move as Matthew got to him.

'My chest,' he said 'can't breathe properly.'

He was covered with blood which streamed from cuts on his head, face and arms. Matthew told him to lay still, and made a dash for an old tarpaulin and first aid kit which was under the passenger seat in the Landrover. He found the tarpaulin, torn and covered in oil. He couldn't find the first aid kit.

He ran back to Steve, who was trying to prop himself up on one elbow.

'Here', said Matthew 'you'd be better off lying still lad, and keeping yourself warm, that's the most important thing. Look, I'm gonna cover you over with this, it's a bit dirty but it will keep you warm.'

He covered Steve with the tarpaulin and Steve began speaking: 'What about my girlfriend, is she okay?'

'Yes, I think so, better than you think probably; I think she may have a broken leg but she's going to be alright. This was my fault and I'm going to make sure you get out of it alright! You're American are you?'

'Yeah', said Steve, 'it's a long way to come for an accident!'.

'Now promise me you'll keep still, it's bad if you move around you see' said Matthew, 'I'm gonna go and get help.'

He jumped in the Landrover and drove to the farm where he dialled emergency for an ambulance, made a flask of sweet tea, collected together some blankets and bandages, before heading back.

'Jesus!' he thought to himself as he approached the couple, 'they must really be in love!'

The girl had dragged herself across the ground to be near Steve, and they were holding each other. Considering what they must have looked like to each other, they were pretty cool. They both managed a 'Hi!' as Matthew approached carrying blankets. As he put a blanket over the girl he saw a bone poking through her bruised and bleeding skin. The pain must have been incredible.

'It was an accident' said Steve 'not your fault.'

He thought of that wet night on the cliffs, Paul's face, and the way the glass had moved across the table. The words of the 'spirit' echoed round his mind, 'Do not drive the yellow car.'

✳

After being in casualty for a few days, Jay was able to be moved and she ended up in a hospital near her parents. Steve stayed in for twenty four hours and was then released, suffering from severe cuts, bruises and some cracked ribs.

The nurses liked him, they liked his sense of humour in the face of pain. He reminded one or two of the older ones of the American boys in Word War II. He had the same charm, the same good looks.

✳

Jay had broken her right leg in two places, and one fracture was close to the pelvis. A few weeks passed, the wound became infected but the hospital staff were unaware of it.

'It bloody hurts like hell!' she said to the staff nurse.

'They all hurt like that dear.' was the stock reply.

Eventually she was taken back into theatre where they discovered an infection, caused by the body's unwillingness to accept the metal which had been inserted into the bone. The metal was removed and a new piece put back in. During one of the operations she remained partially conscious and was aware of the scalpel's incision, the burning sensation, conversations between the staff in the theatre.

'You can't feel anything under anaesthesia.' the

anaesthetist said. 'Believe me, we have had one or two patient's claiming to feel things and hear voices, but that's not unusual when you are under.'

Luckily the infection cleared up, and she was able to move around on crutches. The experience had made her more introverted, she read a lot, and as the weeks ticked by she didn't really come out of herself. Steve came to see her as often as he could, but she was convalescing at her parents' home, he had nowhere to stay, and they both felt uncomfortable.

Matthew Treggiar became a regular visitor, bringing fruit, home-made cake, pictures of his wife and son, and some books by Herman Hesse. He invited Jay to go and stay with his family in their cottage, which she did for a few weeks, before going back to her parents, old friends and the life she knew before.

As the months went by Steve felt their love fading away. The thought of Paul, the seance and what appeared to be a sort of curse weighed heavily on him. He wondered if Paul had cursed them as well.

He became more restless. He surfed as often as he could with Mike, and it helped him deal with the feelings of guilt and the breaking up of the relationship. He read as many books as he could get hold of on hexes and the occult, trying to come to terms with what had happened, the seance and Paul. Who was Paul? He was there and he wasn't there, he weaved his magic and then disappeared.

When telling them about India once he half let it slip that he had gone up into Burma, Thailand and Laos.

Steve and Mike weren't quite sure whether to believe him. He also said that the Vietnam War started in the 1950's, as early as 1954, that actually there had been two Vietnam wars, the Americans became involved when the French were slaughtered at Dienbienphu in 1954. He told them that Vietcong was a name invented by the Americans, and that there had always been Vietnamese fighting for their freedom. When Jack Kennedy was only a Senator, America was already poking its finger into the Vietnamese pie. Paul said it was the C.I.A. who were responsible for imposing Diem on the Government in Saigon, 'Pax Americana is really a replacement of British Imperialism'.

'So have you ever been to Vietnam then Paul?' asked Mike.

'No' said Paul blandly, 'but you'd love it!'

In August the big rock festivals came, the usual chaos of bands, vans, beads, bangles, and trenches to shit in. Mike went off alone to see Hendrix, Steve agreed to join him a few days later at another festival. He thought that afterwards they would get some money together and go surfing, he might show Mike around home, go up the coast to Northern California and the Redwoods.

The second night of the festival Mike was walking along by the stage where the band Judas Priest were playing. Mike was with the 'Leaf Man'. Leaf Man had got his nickname earlier in the summer when he had come back one day from sitting stoned on acid by the stream that ran close to the house where Mike and Steve lived. He had spent several hours willing the leaves to float in particular directions across the stream. Having an interest in lunatics like this, Mike was hanging around with him in a casual sort of a way. Now, as they were walking along, Mike spotted and picked up a plastic bag of purple microdot LSD – the most powerful acid around. The little bag contained enough to blow their brains out for the rest of their lives, which, in Mike's case, is what it did.

'Leaf Man' and Mike both took one of the microdots on the spot and, an hour later, existing festival mayhem transformed into a world where Brueghel and Bosch met the monsters of rock.

Amongst this, Leaf Man cast Mike as a leaf on his stream. Mike began to feel his gaze burning into him. Was he paranoid? It didn't feel like it. Leaf Man was like an embryonic Manson, out for recruits and Mike was stuck there for eight hours at least, this baby psychopath his only companion. He avoided his stare.

People were gathered in small groups around fires, sucking at joints and chillums. One or two couples were rolling around, half clothed or naked. Leaf Man stood silent, still staring into Mike's face, his eyes were like black holes. Mike carried on avoiding him, and edged towards the van he called home, but he was a million light years from there.

The grass beneath his feet seemed to sparkle like a bed of jewels. He looked up at the Leaf Man, 'I'm splitting for a while. See you later.' He turned and walked towards a distant fire where he had made his camp.

A dog snapped at his heels, he put out his hand but the dog cried like a lost spirit. He stopped to stroke it, and they walked on together for a while, but the dog scurried off as they approached Mike's camp.

Near the fire he felt the gaze of a blonde girl who was standing naked except for a grey army coat draped across her shoulders. She looked like a rebel surveying the fires as Dixie burned. She seemed to beckon Mike. Behind was her Volkswagen van, its inside was carefully painted like a gypsy caravan.

The grass changed to mud, cracked and dry like an old river bed. He was spurred on by the need for sanctuary, away from the rabble hoard gathered on its banks, beating their drums and dancing naked. The blonde spoke 'Are you okay?'

Ah, the Grand Inquisitor, The Universal Drug Council. How did she know? He didn't look any different, did he? Maybe the eyes, she must have met the 'Leaf Man', what had he told her?

'I need to rest' Mike said.

'Oh, you can sit in my van for a while if you want, there's nobody in there.'

A life line. 'Yeah. Yeah, thanks.'

Mike followed her to the van.

'If you want anything, just shout, or come on over, we're just over there', and she wandered back to the fire, smiling. He was really spaced. He felt as if he had the strength of an army of devils, his tongue was black and his eyes were red, he was on fire. Everywhere he looked gargoyles and demons looked back, the walls and floors of the van exploded and reformed, snakes crawled over the bed and changed into other animals. Where did they come from? Where were they going? Outside the rabble horde, inside the devil. He had to get back to the ocean.

He opened the door of the van and saw the blonde, the great coat draped across her shoulders.

'Hi, how's it going?'

'Okay. I wanna go surfing.'

'Oh yeah? I hear the waves are pretty good?'

'Yeah.'

'I, I need to find a phone.'

'Why don't you sit down by our fire and relax for a while, and then maybe we can go for a drive, see if we can find a phone in the village or something?'

And so Mike sat. Staring into the embers, he saw gargoyles play in red and black canyons; cities were raised to the ground and then reappeared, their domes glistened in the orange sun. Aztec chiefs grew large and small, their skins a millennium of rivers and creeks. Battles were fought, civilizations came and went, generals gazed upon the destruction they caused.

A pale dancer weaved her way amongst the ruins with thick red lips above heavy dark breasts, she danced frail and beautiful across these scarred lands and for a while she graced them with the holiness of the Madonna.

''Ere mate, grab hold of this!' Mike turned looking

22

straight into the face of Black Rick; Rick was a long way from the round glasses brigade, he was death and glamour. Mike liked him. He passed Mike an enormous joint. It tasted good and it took Mike away from the dancing girl.

'I 'ere you like a bit of surfing pal.' Rick said. 'You've got a mate over here, 'aven't you, from L.A.?'

How does he know that? Mike stared back blankly.

'L.A.?'

'Yeah, Los Angeles. I like the Angels myself.' laughed Rick, 'might even prospect one day!' Mike passed him back the joint.

'See you later, I'm gonna to sit in the van for a while.' He moved off among the debris of bodies and fires, towards the V.W., the mosaics, devils and dancers who waited there for him.

'Hi!' It was Steve. 'Sorry it took so long, I've got this thing going with … ah … someone, you know, I think it's love!'

'Hi. I'm fucking freaked!'

'Yeah?'

'I took … ah … ah some acid with that guy, you know, 'Leaf Man', he's mad, thinks he's Charlie Manson!'

'Right. Got any more acid? I'm running underneath you, I'd better drop some and catch up!'

'Don't take this shit man! Get something off Golden Hair, she's got some Californian Sunshine, on blotter.'

'Um.. well do you want to go up the coast then, surf a bit? The wind's offshore, should be some swell too!'

His friend was so cool, so laid back, so reassuring.

'Yeah! Did you bring the boards?'

'Do hippies shit in the woods? Let's get the fuck out of here!'

Inside the van Mike sat close to Steve. His friend smelt good, like a furry animal. The road up to the coast was joined with the same one Steve and Jay had taken when Matthew Treggiar had altered the pattern of their lives by leaving his plug spanner behind.

Mike stared at a blue and yellow K.P nut packet left on the dashboard, and watched it form into a cobra in 3D, leering and swaying in time with the van and the radio. The acid was still doing its stuff. Steve began to speak.

'I met this guy from San Francisco, he used to juice up on acid and ride his bike up and down the Golden Gate Bridge. I hitched up to Vancouver with him. One morning early we were sitting in the train station in the Mid West, near Colorado, and these cops came in and kicked my feet off the seat. Anyway, I put my feet back up and the cops fucked off. Then four of them came back, dragged us down town, made us strip off and locked us up, the guy I was with was tripping, you know!'

'Easy Rider or what!' Steve glanced across at his friend.

'Yeah.'

They arrived at the top of the cliffs overlooking the ocean, a five or six foot swell was peaking beneath a moderate offshore breeze. The walls of glass they had dreamed about and waited for had appeared, and were beginning to peel off left and right out near the rocks. The sun was low in the early evening sky.

'I've never surfed on acid!'

'Ah, you'll be okay, give you loads of energy!' Steve punched Mike lightly and grinned.

And so began Mike's audience with God. The waves fragmented slowly around him as he paddled out between sets away from the peaks; once outside, his eyes fixed on the red horizon waiting for the wave that would be his. They were coming in sets of six or eight, and he went for the third or fourth.

He took off on a moving six foot mirror, leaving his insides somewhere out on the horizon. He hit the bottom and turned back up towards the curl that was splitting into silver and red and gold beneath the sun. He cut back half way down and back up again, tracing a long smooth line towards the lip which was still slowly peeling right towards the rocks. As he cut across like a diamond on glass he stalled slightly and crouched down so the curl covered him up. There was complete silence, and he was surrounded by the tube of the wave, deep within the green room. It lasted forever. He shot out the other end and zigged up the face, where his stomach caught up with him. He kicked out over the back to land on the dark blue water reflecting the rocks close by.

Saturn hung like Mars, red above the ocean where he lay, gazing as the beautiful planet moved slowly round. The light rays beamed across its surface, indigo, blue, violet and gold, deep into the evening, and deep into the depths of his soul.

The Black Mountains

*A*LAN WALDEN had the face of a warrior king. In Africa for twenty years he had carved out a living from the arid earth until the birth of his third son made him think hard about the future of his adopted country.

He began to feel uncomfortable at cocktail parties on the cream verandas, he had learnt that the white man had a great deal to learn from the black man. As he listened to the chit chat amid the clinking of glasses, he began to doubt that the whites would ever learn, he feared they would let Africa bleed into the next century as she struggled to find herself.

Still, for some years, his heart swelled as his youngest son Michael grew. He struggled hard not to let this little one become his favourite as he watched him walk barefoot with his black friends to play with nothing but a few sticks.

On his seventh birthday Alan gave him a German Shepherd puppy, 'to love and protect', and the dog put to shame the most loyal of friends. Michael cycled to school and the dog ran beside him, ran back to the farm when he was safely inside the school compound and back again to collect him at four o'clock.

'I swear I can tell the time by that bloody dog!' Alan said smiling as the dog sped off, loping wolf-like towards the school in the late afternoon.

In the evenings Mike's mother, Joan, would tell him stories about England and the home they had there a long time ago before he was born. She told him about fir trees heavy with snow, robins and red pillar boxes. In his mind the snow mixed with the stars of the African night and when his mother told him one day that they might return to this land where there were icicles and snowmen he became very excited, very keen to go there. But Africa was paradise, and later, when his parents moved back to England, paradise was lost.

They bought a house in the southern home counties, his father continued working for the same company up in town, in London. Michael went to boarding school with its irrepressible smell of institutions which never left him. It was an unhappy experience, and he never really settled. He thought back to his black friends in Africa, everybody knew everybody and seemed to help each other in the daily struggle. He got through at school because he was good at sport. Few of the teachers were inspirational, but one, 'Duchy', persuaded him to read some history and books which only made him want to leave even more. He was caned by his housemaster for 'constant and deliberate lack of effort'.

'Walden, you are persistently verging on insolence boy! You deserve to be beaten and you will be, until you realise this is not a game!'

'Sir.'

Like all school boys, Mike had learnt the art of feigned surprise and ignorance, how to steer one word, in itself meaninglessly polite, to become an insult.

'Stand up straight boy!'

'Sir'

'Damn you boy!'

They both knew that for 'Sir' he should read 'Prick'. Mike figured it was worth six of the best, which is what he got. He put vaseline on the cuts to stop the cotton from his underpants sticking to the blood, and went for a walk, 'to walk it off.' He was consistent with his attitude, and he quietly became a bit of a hero with the other boys. He had been caned more than any of them, but wouldn't give in. When the time came to leave school both sides were delighted.

He met the American, Steve, six months later in Notting Hill. In those days some of the Jamaicans still wore pork pie hats, still listened to ska, wore suits and liked England. You could stay up all night on the speed in nasal inhalers. Clubs came and went. By and large though the white rock monster rolled down the streets, and the clubs were full of freaks and black men into reggae and plenty of Ghanja.

'It's a bit like the Village!' said the American as he looked at the quiet open-faced English boy opposite him as he rolled a joint.

'What Village?'

'Hell man, Greenwich Village! You know, New York.'

'Oh yeah.' said the English boy blandly. He passed him the joint.

'Want some?'

'I can't really smoke all that tobacco you guys smoke over here. Here, why don't you try some of this? That's Californian grass man, I brought it all the way over with me from back home.'

'You're lucky you got to smoke some of it, you're not stuck in some poxy jail.'

'So what you doing over here then?'

'Well, I'm doing a bit of travelling and hoping to do some surfing, you know, that's my thing.'

'Yeah? You need to go down to Cornwall, that's where all the surf is.'

'You wanna show me how to get there? I've gotta van, an old V Dub, it goes alright.' Mike felt he had nothing to lose, the city was hot and he'd never been surfing.

'Why not?' he grinned.

And that was how they became friends, how Mike started to surf.

When Mike's father had retired he went back to the Black Mountains in Wales because on a good day as the sun set, it reminded him of Africa. As he watched Michael grow into a man he was reminded of himself, but Mike was more detached, rootless. He spent too long alone. Alan had last seen him when he came down to collect some things before going off surfing. After the trip with 'Leaf Man', he knew things weren't right, but Mike didn't want to talk about it.

In the evenings Alan used to sit on his porch with a beer, looking out over the mountains. His wife Joan often sat next to him with a pink gin, it was a habit from Africa. On an evening like this she felt disturbed, uncomfortable. She got up and went inside the house.

'Are you alright darling?'

'Yes, I'm fine. I just feel a little strange, I need to go and sit inside for a little while, you stay out here and finish your beer' she said, smiling.

She went inside and made her way upstairs towards their bedroom. On the way she passed by Michael's room, opened the door and went in. She felt overcome by grief and sadness, for no apparent reason.

Although it was her son's room, it was foreign to her. He slept on a mattress on the floor, the room was sparse, lit by a brightly coloured Mexican blanket for a bed cover, some posters of Jimi Hendrix and Hindu gods on the walls. A small Buddha faced inwards from the window.

As she stood looking and wondering about Mike, she felt a hand on her shoulder and turned, she thought Alan must have come quietly up the stairs to check on her, to see if she was alright. But it was not Alan who was there, it was Michael. He was standing behind her, in a torn shirt and jeans, looking at her.

'Mike ... ?'

Then he disappeared, he was no longer there. she was overcome with distress and sat down on the cushions near the window, and cried.

4

The Last Wave Goodbye

*M*IKE never really came down from the trip with the 'Leaf Man'. Surfing had helped him chill out, but something in his brain made him flash back and begin to trip again. It was terrifying. Drugs were temporary, but this was permanent and over the weeks and months that began to tick by, flashbacks became an integral part of his mental circuits. Wires had got crossed or burnt out, and sometimes, with no warning, he would just become someone else. This someone else was a Buddhist warrior, a monk, and out of the blue Mike used to say something like:-

'Tozan' said Ungan, 'master, if someone asks me a hundred years afterwards what I thought was your deepest understanding, what should I say?'

Ungan answered, 'tell him I said, it is simply this …' Tozan was silent for a time and Ungan said, 'kai, if you have grasped this you must carry it out in detail!'

'In life the rain falls on the just and the unjust. In this the temple of life, to be really alive we must die daily, and be resurrected. To bury a dead man is a waste of time, it's really the living who must gain their life by losing it.' He'd read it, and memorized it, more or less word for word.

The East began to lure him. Yet, at the same time, he was tempted to go West, to California.

'All those beautiful women! All those good waves!' He talked about it and would laugh saying 'I've got splitzophrenia, I'm fucking crazy!'

'I'll tell you what' said Steve 'let's make some money. You get a stash and you can decide where you want to go. Of course if you wanna go home, I mean back to the States, I'd go with you!

'Ah you just wanna go and get into all those Californian girls man! I know what you're like, you come on with all this spiritual stuff about the surf and everything, but at the end of the day you're a buns and burger man! So how are we going to make all this money then?'

'Well, you know, there is this little scam in V.W.'s from Amsterdam. Or near there anyway, you can get buses there, bring them back over here and sell them on for a profit.'

'So you wanna go to Amsterdam then?'

'Yeah!'

'That's just so you can go over there and wander around and get stoned.'

'No, I'm serious, we can do it!' And so it was decided. They went.

Amsterdam was barefoot in Wandel Park, the Orange Julius, in the cafes smoking big chillums of black dope with hairy Dutch and Germans all going on about 'India Man'. The cops left everyone alone, smoking joints, dealing on the streets. It was hot. They were very stoned, the sun hung in an orange glow over the lake in Wandel Park.

To buy the V.W. vans they went to a big car auction near Utrecht; there were Citroens, Mercs, Renaults, Peugeots and V.W. vans all on a huge tarmac square.

'It's just like back home!' said Steve.

'What do you mean?' said Mike.

'It's such a huge auction, you know, they really go for it these guys don't they?!'

'Someone once told me that all the Dutch ever want is their ten percent, what do you think?'

'Ah, dunno! Look, that guy there, he's got a split screen and a new shape, may be we could get them both at a discount!'

They did. Then they drove back into the Dam, bought some black hash and after two huge joints began on the road back to the U.K.

They passed through the small village of Gravelines, by the signs up to the Allied cemeteries. They were quiet.

They drove out of Gravelines to the docks at Calais, crossed over from Calais to Dover and drove back to the edge of the moor where they camped out. They got stoned, lit a fire and the stars lit up the sky.

'You decided what you're going to do when you've sold your van?' asked Steve.

'Yeah, I'm gonna pay back the money you lent me

then I'm gonna spend the rest on drugs.'

'That's a good plan. Have you been thinking of that for a long time?'

'Well yeah, you know, since we were over in the 'Dam.'

Steve laughed and guzzled some wine they had picked up on the way through France. 'Seriously, what are you gonna do?'

'I'm gonna go and see my Mum and Dad. To say goodbye.'

'You gonna hitch?'

'Nah. I'll get the train. I'm not hitching, no one ever stops for me!

The fire burned bright through the night and they slept out until the rising sun cast its light over the first waves they saw on the distant horizon. Small sets came in, three to four feet, and they had them all to themselves.

✳

A week later Mike got up, told everyone he was leaving and went to the train station. It was hot, humid with the smell of diesel in the air. He imagined the old station in its Victorian glory, smoke hung like a veil across the face of the station clock. He was singing, *Voodoo Chile* as he waited for the train.

He couldn't remember all the words, but he knew Hendrix couldn't escape either. Broken glass was all around.

The train pulled in the station. He found a carriage and a place to sit which was not too crowded. Fifteen minutes later, he was looking out of the window onto green fields and lush countryside. He thought back to his childhood, to the bush. He felt the taste of acid in his saliva, adrenaline was starting to pump through his blood. There was no special reason for it, but he thought that another 'attack', which is what he now called them, was on the way. Sometimes he had managed to quieten them down by taking large amounts of Vitamin B, but he had none with him.

He began to breathe in slowly through the tip of his nose, following the breath past his throat and into his lungs, holding it and repeating the cycle. No good. The edge of the olive green seat opposite began to undulate and he now knew why hell was full of serpents.

A middle-aged smartly dressed woman blustered into the carriage and sat down opposite him. He looked up, into dark eyes staring at him. He stared back, and the eyes looked away. *Voodoo Chile.*

The arm of the green seat next to the woman changed into a small dog's head, and this time it was Mike who looked away. He'd had enough, the warrior monk. An honourable harikari?

He got up slowly and took off his shirt. He put the palms of his hands together, turned to the four points of the compass and then leaned back, his face parallel with the ceiling of the carriage. Earth, air, fire and water. He was now deep in the temple of a black Buddha. He closed his eyes. He was standing between two perfectly straight lines of Buddhas, and he walked slowly down the aisle between them. At the end was the most beautiful one of all. It was emerald, and incense burned nearby. A monk in saffron robes stood behind the Buddha, beckoning, and Mike stepped forward, reaching out to him. Suddenly there was nothing beneath his feet, and he was gripped with fear. The monk had gone and he was alone in the dark. He began to feel pain, a burning through his flesh. It eventually stopped, and he seemed to be in the air about two metres above his body which was frying on the tracks below him.

Then he was standing behind his mother in his bedroom. The room was empty, apart from her and his few belongings. His brightly coloured Mexican blanket was now different shades of black and white, and his mother was grey, it was as if he was locked inside an old black and white film, watching and being part of the set with no control or direction. He reached forward to touch his mother on the shoulder. He could feel nothing but she did turn, and for a second he thought that she recognized him, she could see him. Then he was gone, into the sponge-like greyness that surrounded him.

Rolling Thunder

*T*IME PASSED SLOWLY for Steve after the news of Mike's death. What had once been light grew dark; he surfed alone, paddling out in the morning like a lonely dolphin.

The night he heard that Mike was dead he travelled to where they had camped out, and lit a fire in the night as a kind of beacon. The fire burned and his soul burned with it. Hot and bothered, he struggled to find some peace as the cool hands of the night laid him down to rest.

After things with Jay had broken down he had been spending his time with an Irish girl. She took no shit.

'I've been thinking' he began lazily.

'Don't damage yourself' she said.

'Yeah, well as I was saying, I've been thinking about getting a bike.'

'Well, if you ride that bike like you drive a car, sure, we'd all be dead in a few minutes!'

'Come on! I know where there's a Bonneville, I always wanted a British bike, it's been customized a bit but its great, you know, bits of chrome here and there – you'd love it!'

'Yeah, and I suppose you're gonna take that board of yours on it all the way up to the surf now are you?'

'Yeah, well there is a bit of a problem there, but guys back home used to have side bars on their bikes, you know, Harleys, you can stick a board on them and stuff.'

'Ah sure, and it must be lovely in the rain!'

'Well anyway, the surf's up, do you wanna come up with me?'

'No. I said I'd help out doing some cooking at Harry's. You know, that guy he's got there, said he could bake bread, using all that organic flour and stuff. Well it turned out like planks of wood so I said I'd go and give him a hand.'

'Show him how it's done eh?' smiled Steve.

'Aye. And don't you be coming in there with your surfing mates thinking you can be scrounging food for nothing. The only folks we feed for nothing are those who can't afford it, and that's not you, mr. international car dealer now is it!'

'Er, you forgot the surf star bit!'

'Ah, get out of here now, get away wicha!'

He walked over to her putting his arms around her, kissed her hard on the mouth, his hands beginning to wander down her back and over the curves of her ass. She pushed him off lightly, smiling and laughing.

'Go on now, you know you'd rather be there playing in those waves.'

He kissed her again. 'I've gotta get my head together, you know.'

'Aye, I know.'

He parked up on the cliffs to watch the sets roll in. He had to steel himself to get into his wetsuit and paddle out. The waves were not particularly good, but he never blamed the waves. The wind had swung around slightly so that sections that once held up would now be hard to make. It was difficult to get outside, the lulls were few and far between. He took off on the first wave that looked half decent, crouched more on the board and began to trace a series of curves up and down the face. The wind dropped, and the conditions seemed to improve a little.

The sets were getting bigger, and after twenty minutes or so he had to change his marker for the line up. A mist came in and as the waves got even bigger he paddled out further towards the horizon, pleased that the swell had picked up, but feeling a bit apprehensive as he could now hardly see the shore. He turned round to face the horizon and waited for the next set. Surprised by its size, he had to paddle out further and he just managed to crawl up the face of what must have been a twelve to fourteen footer which was beginning to break up. He made it over the top, and gasping for breath, he paddled like never before. Directly behind it was the next in the set and he pushed on to begin his climb up its grizzly face. What was going on?

He thought of turning back to the shore, and tried to find his shore marker, hoping that the mist might have cleared up around it. He knew he had to keep on paddling to get outside, get away from danger and try and take off on a wave to bring him in. Where were the rocks? He wasn't sure, he couldn't see.

Sometimes in the winter at home the Californian surf got big and hairy, but he had never experienced a swell changing as quickly as this. The waves seemed to grow set by set, and conditions on the shore had changed radically. His heart was pumping, fear pushing the adrenaline around his blood like the pump in an over-heated engine.

'The way I see it, it's all like one big radiator', said Captain Beefheart. Steve, for some reason, thought of the last gig by the Captain in L.A., cloaked in black he prowled the stage like a panther from hell.

He was going to have to take a wave. His strength had gone, he would have to take the next one, before it took him. It lurched out of the mist and rolled towards him, its shape all but gone as the wind had now swung round fully, driving these monsters across the ocean like tanks across the desert.

He turned his board with its nose towards the shore and waited for the right moment to paddle like crazy onto the beast, onto its shiny body that could at any time roll over and crush him like the speck on the planet's surface that he surely was. He felt the surge beneath him, it was too late to pull out, and he had to go for it. He was hurtling down a moving mountain with really nowhere to go, but he got up to his feet and managed a gentle turn to the right, away from what would have once been the shoulder. He looked along its face to a section which seemed makeable, perhaps luck was after all still with him. He tempted fate again and began to crank his board round on the black face of the monster.

It was suddenly very quiet. Time stood still. He felt as if Mike was surfing with him, and he looked round, expecting to see him, as if he had taken off behind him on the same wave. His friend would then have cut a different track along the wave, like the different paths they cut in life.

The wave was empty, but the presence of his friend was all around. In his mind a voice was saying, 'go for that section now.' Steve trimmed his board, shifted the weight towards the front and speeded up, crouching and hardly moving for what seemed like an eternity. Incredibly the wave held up and he kept his position, using his weight to trace a careful diagonal towards the bottom of the next section with a view to a very cautious turn back up towards the shoulder. A mountain of white water was behind him, and there but for fortune he would have been. The voice said, 'keep going', and again he felt the presence of his friend all around him. He knew the rocks must be close, he had to stay on the wave and he couldn't see. 'Keep going' said Mike. He did.

For a second the mist cleared and he was just able to take a marker from the beach so that he knew the rocks were to his left. If he kept moving he would end up in some deep but still water on the left-hand side of the bay. He trimmed the board again, shifting his weight slightly more towards the nose and crouched down, leaning at the same time into the black water. Like a shooting star in the night he knew neither time nor space.

Burned out, exhausted, he arrived at the left-hand side of the beach, where the depths of a channel forced the waves to reform before they finally threw themselves onto the shore. If he paddled in a straight line and got picked up again by one, smaller now but still six to eight feet, he would simply be dumped badly near the beach. Between the channel and the rest of the bay the white water was manageable, and he began to paddle across towards it. After an eternity, his arms and shoulders almost seized with pain, he was able to pick up a ride in and he finally dragged himself up onto the beach.

'You alright mate? It looked like someone was out to get you there. I thought of going out meself but when I saw you out there I didn't think I'd bother!'. The voice had a heavy Australian drawl, and Steve looked up into the tanned face of a blue eyed Australian.

'It came up a bit quick, never seen anything like that before!'

'Bugger me! You're a Yank ain't ya?'

'Yeah.'

'Yeah, well that figures. I didn't think any Poms would have the balls to go out in that!'

'Oh I don't know. I had a mate who was a Brit. who would have lapped that up!'

Steve thought back to the darkness of the wave, and the presence of his friend.

'Listen mate. Our combie's just over there, do you wanna come round and have a cuppa or something? There's a few of us down 'ere, we heard that it was good, but the trouble with this place is you only get a decent swell when it's bloody freezing!'

Steve smiled, pulled himself together and up onto his feet, picking his board up at the same time. 'Yeah, that'll be great, thanks.'

Hanging around the combie three other Aussies were putting the bags back over their boards and sticking them up on the roof rack. It was freezing cold, they were wearing shorts and sandals. One of them, ginger haired and freckled, turned round and smiled at Steve.

'Jeez, we were just about to go out and have some fun till we saw you disappearing over the falls! Bloody cold down there eh mate?!'

The others laughed, another one began. 'That's why the Poms are always whinging mate, so fucking cold here I don't blame them!'

'This Pom's a Yank mate!'

'Well bugger me!'

'Yeah. All the way from California!'

'I hear the surfs not much better over there!' They all chortled. One of them had a broken coke bottle in his hand, which had been smoothed off around the edges slightly and it was bunged full of grass. He lit it, and it went up like a bonfire. He took a huge toke on it, and then passed it round to his mates. They all took a toke on it and then passed it to Steve. Tea and sympathy were obviously not an option, he took it and sucked it into his lungs. For good measure he took another one, blew the smoke out slowly and passed it back to the first Aussie.

'Thanks!' he said smiling. He had gained silent approval from these hard men.

'My name's Steve by the way.'

'This is Danny, we call him Dingo. That's Ripper, his real name is Rick, that's Sawman – his name's Steve as well and I'm Martin but everyone calls me Masher!'

The dope reached Steve's brain, and the names and introductions floated in and out of his mind. He'd wait until they spoke to each other and catch the names then.

'Reckon we'll get in the combie, smoke a few more chillums and wait for that wind to swing round, eh. Then we'll be nice and stoked for when we go out!' said Ripper, or was it Sawman.

'First decent fucking swell you get here, and the fucking wind's onshore! Next thing is, it'll be pissing with rain! 'Ere Dingo, cop hold of this!'

So that was Dingo. He was about five feet ten and about four feet wide. He had a boyish face, but two of his front teeth were missing which detracted from his otherwise good looking features. Dingo took a massive toke on the broken coke bottle. ''Ere Ripper' he gasped. 'Stoke up on this mate!'

Dingo looked at Steve. 'Fancy a cup of tea mate?'

'Yeah! Thanks very much, that would be great!'

Ripper was taller than Dingo, and not as big, he was only about three and a half feet wide. He was still wearing his wetsuit, a long john, and his arms hung down the side of them, about the size of Steve's thighs. Ripper too had good looking features which were at odds with his body. He turned to Steve 'You alright mate?' He had felt Steve's eyes on him.

'Yeah.' He was really stoned now. 'Just mellowing out man, you know.' The laid back Californian.

'You always surf alone mate?' said Martin, Masher.

Steve flashed back to the big wave, to Mike surfing it with him, guiding his mind through the sections that were unmakeable. Hexes, Paul, the crash and his friend's death almost took a physical hold of him.

'Uh, well, you know, back home, there used to be a lot of guys that used to go out, you know. I came over here to get some quieter waves!' he said smiling quietly.

'Well these are so fucking quiet there's no one out there!' Ripper was laughing, and Dingo joined in.

'You did good out there though mate! We were rooting for you, y'know, never thought you'd make that last section, but looked like you knew exactly where you were going!'

'Ah it was luck, you know, really. I just closed my eyes and went for it!'

''Ere mate, have some of this.'

It was Sawman passing Steve the coke bottle burning like a torch and hot as hell.

An hour or so later, his brain feeling like a marshmallow, Steve left the combie and made his way back to Kate.

'It's always a Sheila gets between a bloke and his

mates!' laughed Dingo.

'Hope she's worth it!'

'Tell you what, why don't you and her stop by tomorrow. We're gonna have a bar-bie on the beach, rain or snow!' said Ripper.

'Yeah, cool. I'm a veggie, so I'll bring some stuff with me, okay?'

'Cool!' it was Martin. 'Dingo used to be a veggie, didn't you Dingo! Then he reckons one day just up north of Wollongong he went inland, broke down and ended up eating roo steaks. He fucking loved them! Never looked back, have you Ripper!'

Ripper looked slightly sheepish. 'Nothing like a roo steak mate! Anyway we'll see you up here tomorrow! Why don't you come up early if the wind's dropped, go out for a few waves, eh?'

'Yeah. See you then!' Steve left.

'Jesus! Look at the state of you! You look like the wreck of the Hespers!'

'What the fuck does that mean?'

'Ah well, it was something my mother used to say when I'd come in of an evening!' Kate started giggling, reminiscing obviously, of drunken nights in Belfast.

'I met some Aussie guys so had a smoke with them after the surf. They're nice guys, you know, I said we'd maybe pop round and see them tomorrow if the surf is up and they invited us for a bar-bie. Do you feel like doing that?'

'Sure, why not! Make a change some of your surf mates cooking for me instead of me cooking for them now!'

'Kiss?' she walked up to him and they met in the middle of the room, he put his arms round her waist and pulled her tight to him. She had reached up towards him, and they kissed for a long time. He slipped his hands up her back, round onto her breasts.

Chainsaw Charlie

YOU KNOW, I never told you but when I was out there in that surf I felt like Mike was surfing with me, I mean that he was really there!'

'Well, we often feel that people who have just died are still with us. Do you want some of this?' She was rolling a joint, a mixture of grass and hash. 'If you do, I'll put some more grass in it.'

'No thanks. Its clear light and beauty for me now all the way!'

'Yeah?'

'Look, what I am saying is I thought that he was, you know, really there. Maybe he is trying to tell me something, maybe because of the way he died he's not really at rest, what do you think?'

'Well, they say back home that if you take your own life then the soul is never at rest and sure now there were lots of old priests who used to talk about poltergeists and possession and be sprinkling the holy water everywhere!'

'Yeah, but did it work?'

'Aye, it must have done, because there are more ghosts in England than there are in Ireland!'

'Look, stop screwing around, I'm serious! What do you really think?'

'Well, I know there's an Irish priest come to live over here 'cause my mate Sarah was talking about him, funnily enough they were talking about hearing a baby cry in the attic in this old house they've just moved into. It disturbed her so much and they called this old fella in, and they played a tape and recorded the sound of the baby crying but they never saw anything.'

'You're pulling my chain!'

'No, really it's true! Apparently this fella receives quite a few calls every year from folk who are worried about that sort of thing, you know, poltergeists and hauntings and that .'

'Well, what do you think? Do you think Mike's not at rest, I mean ...'

'I dunno Steve. Why don't you go and see this old fella now and have a chat with him? Maybe he could put your mind at rest, help you out, and he could say a prayer for Mike, you never know, can't do any harm now can it?!'

She took a large toke on the joint she had rolled for herself and smiled, raising her eyebrows to Steve, silently asking him if he wanted to change his mind. He shook his head.

Three days later, in the evening, Steve was walking under an old iron bridge up along a narrow street towards a small timber framed cottage where the priest lived. Good as her word, Kate's friend had got in touch with him, and he was only too willing to 'have a chat.' It was raining, and he felt cold in just his t-shirt.

Father Tom Wallace was chubby, late middle-aged with white hair and a cheerful round smiling face. In the half light of the porch, as he asked Steve in, his kindliness beguiled the hidden depths of piercing blue eyes, they had a look of quiet resilience, like an old general who had seen many battles, who took on the enemy and believed that with God on his side he could win.

'Well now, come on in and sit yourself down! You're soaking wet for goodness sake, I was just about to have a wee dram myself, would you like to try some of this?' Father Wallace held up a dark brown bottle which Steve failed to recognise.

'Oh of course now, yes, your girlfriend, or was it her friend, told me you are an American fella aren't you? You wouldn't perhaps have this over there, well not too much of it anyway! It is what we call a single malt, it's for warming the soul on nights like these!' The priest smiled warmly, weighing up his young guest.

'Yes, thank you, I would like to try some.'

'So, your girlfriend is from Belfast. Not too far away from where I come from! And where is it in America that you are from, young man?'

'Well Father, my family's from the Mid West but I spend most of my time in California'.

'Ah yes, a lovely part of the world! We have relations out there of course.'

'Well, I think there's Irish blood in me sir, on my mother's side.'

'Aye, if it's in your blood then that's not a bad thing! So what is it that's troubling you? Sarah, Kate's friend, was saying you feel you may have a friend who is perhaps not at peace?' He passed Steve some of the malt in a large glass.

'We've had a strange time, I mean we had a strange time. We met this guy who was a very powerful sort of character, we sort of fooled around with a seance, and I don't know, but it seems we conjured something up and well, I had a car crash afterwards, split up with my girlfriend and it's all kind of been a whole mess'.

'Go on.'

'Yeah, well as I was saying, we had this seance and we were hanging out with – Paul – this guy and my friend just sort of flipped out and thought he was some sort of reincarnation of a monk and stuff like that. We spent a lot of time trying to get him to get his head together, but I'd kind of be talking to him and he'd be normal and then like another minute he would grab hold of me like he was somebody else, like he was possessed or something. Anyway, sometime ago, about three weeks or so ago, he killed himself and I had to go and talk to his folks an' all and, well, his ma saw him in his bedroom at the time of his death. And the other day I was out in some really big surf, like the swell seemed to come up from nowhere, and then it was as if my buddy, the one who killed himself, was surfing with me. I mean that he was really with me, not like I thought he was with me, but like he was there! I was talking it over with Kate, you know, and she said you might be able to help me or help him or whatever.'

Father Wallace smiled, as if surveying the distant hills with a view to a flanking movement.

'Well now, the first thing is, you mustn't be embarrassed or ashamed by what you are thinking or what you have told me. A lot of people have come across these sort of problems and most of them keep them to themselves. But I tell you now evil is there and it can flatten us. If you go against it on your own it will crush you as surely as you crush an ant, but if you take God with you, then of course you have nothing to fear.'

Steve took a gulp of his whisky and felt it warming his gullet. He looked into the eyes of the priest and started to believe. The Father continued. 'There are people on this earth who have strange powers, and it sounds like your old friend, Paul is it?, may have had some kind of connection with the darker side, possibly unknowingly, although that is doubtful. He may have influenced you but from what you are saying and the way you are, I don't think any harm has come to you. But your young friend, the one who has killed himself, he is altogether in a different situation. I think between us we must do our best to help him. I take it you are not what you might call a Christian, young man?'

Steve shuffled, looked down and then up, back into the eyes of the Father. He began speaking before Steve. 'Ah, I see that you are not! Well, never mind, the good thing is that your soul will be in the right place and our

Lord takes a very broad view of his children.' The Father smiled and Steve felt more at ease. 'Do you believe in anything?'

'Well, we got pretty into the Far East, we read a lot about Buddha. Paul had spent some time out in India and he had some really weird tales of what those guys do, and, well, we got really into all that sort of thing.'

'Ah well now, I wouldn't say that Buddha and Christ were too far apart at all! In fact, you might argue they are one and the same, but seen from different points of view. What we'll do now is sprinkle some holy water for your friend and it might help if I perhaps could pay a visit to his parents, if I could be of any use to them, the poor souls! It may be useful also for me to see the spot where he took his life, and the rest you will have to leave up to me.'

'And what about Paul and me? I mean people can't actually curse you or something can they?'

'No, no, no! That's a lot of nonsense that you see on the films and all! No, you carry on and go about your business in the normal way lad, go out and do some of that surfing you like so much, perhaps take that nice Irish girl with you eh?'

'Well, I was thinking of doing a bit of travelling. A lot of my buddies back home are going off to 'Nam an' such, I don't think I'll do that, but I wouldn't mind maybe having a look round India or somewhere. You know my friend Mike, he couldn't ever really decide whether to go out to California or to go to the East. It wouldn't be a bad thing would it if I went to the East?'

'Oh goodness, no, not at all! Why, India and all those beautiful countries will do you some good, maybe put these things out of your mind! Steve took a last slug of the single malt, it burnt his throat and seemed to burn away the fears of Paul, hexes, the darkness which had invaded him since the accident and Mike's death.

'Well, I guess I'd better be going, Thank you Father, thank you for everything, is that it?'

The priest smiled, 'Well as I said before, it is best you leave this up to me now. If you do feel afraid at any time of course, always come and see me. If you feel afraid and you are in one of those foreign places, what you must do is to recite the Lord's prayer. That, you see, in the Church is an exorcism. Every time you recite the Lord's prayer and say 'deliver us from evil' an exorcism is taking place and you will be safe. You do know the Lord's prayer now don't you?'

Steve shuffled again. 'Well yes sir, of course we learnt it, I mean yes, I do know it.'

Father Wallace smiled again, turned and walked to an old bookshelf close to the side of the fireplace where the log fire was still burning bright. He took out a small book with a dark maroon leather cover and handed it to Steve.

'This lad is the book of Common Prayer, it is for common men like us! My father gave it to me when I first took up the Orders, and when you get back from your travels it will give you an excuse to come and see me now, won't it! You can bring it back and tell me all about what has gone on! How does that sound?'

Steve smiled, reached out to take the large powerful hand that the priest held out to him. 'Thank you Father, thank you very much, I'll not let you down!'

'Oh sure now, there's no chance of that now is there, on your way now!'

In the half light of the glowing fire, Steve imagined that the priest had had many a good fight. He wanted to ask him if he believed in ghosts, but thought that perhaps he already knew the answer and turned to leave, to walk back down the small narrow streets in the rain, in the dark.

✳

A week later, the pale winter sun cracked the ice on the cottage windows in the early morning. Thick frost hung on the grass, and the trees stretched like white skeletons against the heavy winter sky. Steve ran his hand down his girlfriend's back, on to her thigh, and back up again. She turned onto her side, opening her eyes slowly, squinting against the morning light that was probing its way into the room, on to the sheets and her skin, still tanned from the long hot summer. Kate smiled and pulled her man towards her, kissing him on the mouth and then on the cheek. 'I have got to get to work you know!'

'Yeah? Why don't you be late?' he said with a smile, pulling her back towards him. She giggled, pushing him off, 'Jesus! I can't now, that would be the third time I've been late this week, and it's only Thursday! You need to go surfing or something, I swear you're gettin' worse! We can fool around tonight though, I'll make sure I don't work late, maybe you could even cook some supper, do you think, could you?'

They kissed. 'Deal!' smiled Steve.

'Any chance of a cup of tea then?'

'Ah well now, God loves a trier, and there's nobody as trying as you!'

Kate rolled away from Steve and guided her feet on to the floor grabbing an old kimono as she went.

'Hmm! Come back!' purred Steve, but she was on her way into the small kitchen to fill the kettle and warm the tea pot under the hot tap.

'Kate, you know Father Wallace thought it wouldn't be a bad idea if maybe I did go out and have a nose round in the East, to put my mind at rest about Mike and that. What do you think, do you think you'd want to come with me?'

'Well now, would you be going for a month or a year?'

'I thought I'd really just go over for a few months, you know, we've always talked about going through Turkey and Afghanistan and everything, that's really a trip I wanna do with you and I think we should take our time. I mean for this I could fly out to Thailand or somewhere and, well, I just have this thing about going to a temple, or finding a monk out there and seeing how he reacts to the story I've got to tell. You know, this bit about Mike being a warrior monk and the Buddhism and stuff. I mean, Father Wallace I think was great and I feel much better now I've been to see him but I still have this nagging feeling. It's Paul, it comes from Paul and I have to sort it out for myself and Mike. I can't figure out why he kept on and he was saying stuff, you know, that was just out of nowhere. It was as if he had been taken over by someone else, and maybe it's only a Buddhist monk who can really put that thing to rest. What do you think?'

'You know what I think. If you want to do something you're going to go and do it anyway, so what's the point in asking me what I think, that's stupid! But don't go out through Afghanistan and into Pakistan. You know, when Jimmy came back last year, it took him a year to get over it.'

She smiled, backlit by the sun through the windows, the best thing that had or ever would happen to the guy, right there in the room.

'Well, I could fly to Bangkok and maybe have a look round there, and go on up to the north of Thailand. I've gotta tell you as well, Kate, there is a thing I have about the war and everything. I gotta letter from Bobby last week and, you know, he's gone and volunteered, I can't believe it! He's at boot camp now, he'll be doing his first tour in 'Nam and then R&R in Thailand.'

'Well, don't you get any funny ideas while you're out there with any of your mates, and joining up! You know, Vietnam, that's a terrible war! Why, if Jack Kennedy had still been President, do you really think the war would be happening there at all?'

'Hell, if Jack Kennedy was still alive a lot of things

wouldn't be happening! C'mon, don't start on that one! I'm not going to go and get drafted or go and join up or anything. I think it's a bad war! I'm just saying baby, a lot of my buddies are over there and it feels kind of strange that's all. I feel a bit like I'm dodging the issues or something. I mean, what if I did get drafted, you know they can send draft papers to me back home?'

'Well, I think that's a bridge you'll have to cross when you come to it. Anyway, if you are going to be out in Thailand for a month or two and then if we are going to go back out through Turkey, it's going to be very hard for you to be pitching up now isn't it, at some boot camp!'

She poured the tea from a dark brown pot into two honey coloured mugs, handing one to Steve 'Here now, perhaps this will get you out of bed!'

'Aw, I was hoping it might get you back in!' He smiled. 'So, what shall I do then? I've still got about a thousand bucks left and, you're working hard all the time, you'll be finished there in a month or so, maybe I should just go for that? A month or so – I don't think I'd want to be away from you for more than a few weeks really!'

'Ah, you smooth talking Yankie boys are all the same! Sure you'll be be saying that to some poor sweet girl in Bangkok in a weeks time, get away with you!' She laughed and pulled on an embroidered cotton top over her long skirt.

'Well, whatever you do' she said 'you'd better hurry up and get on with it! I don't want you whispering about ghosts for the rest of your life. We all loved Mike, but he would want you to get on with your life now! If you think his soul's not at rest and you can help by going out and doing this, then you'd better go and do it. I think Father Wallace would do just as good a job and probably is already, but it wouldn't do any harm now for a Buddhist Monk to hear your story would it?' she smiled.

✳

'Cabin doors to manual please, cabin doors to manual.'

Steve turned and looked at the Indian woman sitting next to him who had joined their flight in Delhi. As she got on the plane he wondered why an Indian woman was flying to Thailand, but thought better of beginning a conversation. She had dark rings beneath her eyes, as if she hadn't slept for a month. A yellow sari seemed to reflect the pallor of her skin, and she carried the fatigue from which all India suffers.

He reached up to grab his small bit of hand luggage from the locker above, and made his way to the front exit. He had been lucky, he had managed to get a seat near an escape exit and got the extra leg-room to stretch out over the long hours from London to Thailand, but as he stepped out into Bangkok airport at three in the afternoon, the heat hit him like an iron bar and he gasped for breath. He recovered, and made his way steadfastly down the steps and through into customs which was a bit like a cattle market. He was travelling light, on flights around the States and over to Europe he had given up the idea of waiting at the luggage carousel, and he was soon through customs into the exit area of the airport.

'Taxi sir, taxi?! Taxi, taxi, taxi!'

This was the first time the American had ventured further east than France. To the pack of taxi drivers at Bangkok he was a lamb strolling quietly across green fields; he looked at the smallest of the drivers who was clutching a brass badge in his hand which reminded him of an English bus conductor's badge. For all he knew it probably was.

'Taxi, taxi sir, taxi! American? Many Americans here, many R&R! You like R&R?'

Steve was bending and melting in the fire. The initial blow of the heat when stepping down from the aircraft was no less severe in the airport terminal; air conditioning was then as remote in Bangkok and as unreachable for most Thais as the centrefold girl of Playboy magazine.

'O.K. taxi.'

'We take you Chinatown, we take you Banglamphu?'

'O.K. Banglamphu!'

'O.K. we go Khaosan Road, you like very much, Khaosan Road!'

So Steve met a tuk-tuk for the first time, the sort of chain-saw powered rickshaw driven by the offspring of kamikaze pilots from World War Two who must have crashed there and mated with locals from the asylum.

Steve slung his small kitbag in beside him and had

hardly sat down when his new friend revved the engine to get it screaming in pain; they hurtled over the sticky tarmac where pedestrians and cyclists moved surrealistically out of his path. The air was heavy with petrol and diesel fumes, the road was full of taxis, tuk-tuks, Thais, Chinese and Farangs, some of whom were tall, tanned young men who looked weary beyond their years, on R&R from Vietnam. The driver pulled up outside a Chinese guest house in Banglamphu, where laundry was hanging over the balcony. Two mongrels who had been lying in the dirt by the front porch jumped up to greet him like a long lost friend. They didn't like Steve, and a brown one with yellow teeth curled his right lip up and over the gums, eyeing him up. His mate came round in a flanking movement to Steve's side and they both leaped at his legs at the same time. Steve jumped back inside the tuk-tuk. The journey, the jet lag and the afternoon heat took their toll; he snapped, jumping down from the right side of the tuk-tuk, and charged at the dogs, swearing. He landed about six inches from them and they turned tail and ran. The driver watched all this and came up to Steve's side.

'50 baht, you give me 50 baht please?!'

Steve looked at him. 'What?'

'50 baht, 50 baht, you give me 50 baht!' The guy was definitely in a groove.

'You told me 20 baht at the airport,' Steve said.

'Banglamphu 50 baht. You give me 50 baht! Please?!'

Steve cast an eye up to the laundry hanging over the balustrade on the top porch, several pairs of eyes were staring down at him. He rummaged in his jeans pocket and pulled out 30 baht, offered it to the driver.

'50 baht, Banglamphu 50 baht, you give me 50 baht!'

'C'mon man, You told me 20 baht from the airport, that's already a rip off I know. Here y'go, here's 30, you take 30, 30 baht, it's good, 30 baht!'

'Okay, give me 40 baht, you give me 40 baht, I go. Give me 40 baht!'

The heat seemed to press down on Steve's head as if someone was applying leverage to the iron bar.

'40 baht, 40 baht! Please?!'

Steve stooped down, picked up his bag, slid it on his back, looked at the driver and hissed, '30 baht, and fuck you!'

Okay! 30 baht. Give me 30 baht!'

'Okay,' Steve smiled, '30 baht!'

He turned back round and walked up the wooden steps into the guest house. From the corner of his left eye he caught a glimpse of one of the dogs eyeing up his legs.

The house was dimly lit and to Steve's eyes, used to the white heat of the outside, as dark as a tomb. An elderly Thai appeared from nowhere and smiled at Steve as the darkness began to change into thin yellow light.

'You want room? Room 50 baht, no fan.'

'What about a shower?'

The old man shuffled off towards a door at the back of the yellow room and beckoned. They went outside again, the heat made fiercer by the renewed intensity of the light. The old man pointed to a dirty pipe leading up to a flaking chrome showerhead mottled with rust. The shower surround was concrete and there was a drain in the left hand corner.

'Shower!'

The old man was smiling, clearly delighted at the quality of the accommodation he was offering.

'30 baht.' said Steve.

The old man must have been one of the pairs of eyes on the balcony which had seen Steve jump from the back of the tuk-tuk just in front of the dogs. He said, 'Okay, 40 baht. No fan.'

'No fan.'

His room was a mattress on the floor in a square of about ten feet, with a small window looking out onto the backyard of the guest house. The yard was the dogs lair. As he looked through the window one of them caught a glimpse of the movement and looked up, making eye contact. They exchanged stares, the dog casually turned his head away to nibble a flea on his hind leg. The other one was lying down in the shadows of a palm.

A skeletal ginger cat walked along the top of the wall above the dogs. To the left of the dogs, a small boy appeared from the alley where the shower was. He saw Steve leaning out of his window, and smiled as he stooped and picked up a stone. Before Steve could say hello, the stone had reached the ginger cat. It lost its grip on the wall and was forced to twist and jump down into the yard, two or three feet in front of the dogs. It sprung back on to the wall before the dogs could get it, and the boy disappeared.

Jet lag was beginning to kick in. Steve rummaged around in his bag, dragged out a towel and washbag and made his way to the shower. It worked. The only source of water was heated by the sun in the pipes and was almost too hot. Back in his room he lay down on the piece of foam and crashed out. Two hours later he woke up, hot and sweating. His room had turned orange, it faced west and the sun was beginning to set. He got up, showered again, put on some jeans, t-shirt and sandals. He secured his money and passport in a belt around his waist and set off for downtown Bangkok.

Out in the street he was overawed by the scent of flowers and oranges which seemed to mix with the colour of the sun. He was in a part of the city between the river and the railway, the old part of Bangkok. He turned right, down a big road which he thought he'd follow, trying to take note of some landmarks along the way to retrace his steps later on. The setting sun bathed the street in a golden light and he felt relaxed. The Thais didn't bother him, they seemed to be going about their business in the early evening, beginning to set up stalls by the side of the road, cooking prawns and chicken on sticks, which some of them were already eating with bowls of sticky rice.

He stopped at a shop, the shop keeper smiled, Steve smiled back and pointed to a small white Buddha. The shop keeper smiled again, nodded his head and lifted the lid of a glass cabinet, retrieving the Buddha. As he handed it to Steve, he smiled, again nodding his head up and down. 'Wat phra keo?' he said. Steve looked blank. The shop keeper tried again. 'Wat?' Steve smiled and nodded. 'What?'. The shop keeper came round from behind the glass cabinet and went towards the front of his shop, which was really a square box of a stall opening straight out onto the street. He pointed to the direction where Steve had been walking. 'Wat, wat phra keo', he said.

The penny dropped. Four hundred metres or so further on, he noticed a large building looming up into the sky, it had a reddish pointed roof supported by tall pillars, turning amber in the early evening. It looked like a palace. He walked on, and stopped by a small dark skinned Thai who was setting up a food stall by the side of the road.

'Wat?' said Steve. The Thai looked up at the Farang and smiled.

'Wat phra keo!' smiled the stall holder, pointing to the tall building.

Steve walked up the steps lined by stone carved figures, across a small terrace and up a narrower set of stairs leading to two large golden doors. He saw shoes outside the doors and took his own off.

He noticed some westerners with some Thais looking at a green Buddha in a glass case. He was drawn towards it and joined them, standing silently to stare at the Buddha seated on a pedestal, high above his head. An aura of mystery engulfed him. He was staring at the

Emerald Buddha, the talisman of the Thai kingdom.

Steve remained in the temple for some time, walking back to look again at scenes from the ramayana painted in murals on the temple walls.

He spent three more days in Bangkok before the traffic, the noise and the heat got too much and he moved on a hundred kilometres or so west, to the Maeklang River which ran the length of the small town of Kanchanaburi. From here he planned to go north up to Changmai. He caught the early train from the Noi railway station and travelled third class. The hard wooden seats and stifling air were more than compensated for by the kindness of the Thais who shared water melons and drinks with him. They thought he was something to do with the war. His hair was too long to be a G.I., but as always rumours coloured the fabric of Farang and Thai relationships, rumours of the CIA using Thailand as a cover to go into the northern hinterland of Vietnam through Cambodia. There were other rumours of drug smuggling from Chiangrai, in the golden triangle between Burma, Northern Thailand and Cambodia. The north attracted him like a magnet. In quieter moments he thought of Mike whose death still weighed heavily on his mind, sometimes the dark cobbled streets of Europe didn't seem so far away. What had happened that night back in the old country on the black edge of time? What had really happened to Mike? What about Paul?

Paul

*T*HE DEATH of Lieutenant Colonel Peter Dewey of the American OSS in Saigon on September 26 1945 was auspicious. He was the first American to die in Vietnam. Paul was born three years later when his French father returned there to marry his exotic and beautiful Vietnamese mistress, Paul's mother. Paul's early years were spent growing up with the French war in Indo China. His father led the life of a privileged colonial, touring the family's rubber plantations, checking the production, his responsibility.

Vietnam was a world of revolution and intrigue. Occasionally this spilled over into the quiet of the white mansion and its gardens where Paul first smelt the potent mix of tropical rains on the sunbaked earth. His father was often away for long periods in France, but when he came back he always returned with presents. He talked about Americans, a thing called television, how the Americans had machines that did the washing, and others that could even wash cars.

On the plantation the days passed slowly. There was

a routine, but Paul didn't notice it, he gazed upwards through the dark green foliage of the rubber trees to the blue sky beyond. On the ground he watched the ants amass their troops like the Vietminh at Dienbienphu, he played in the dirt with them, burned their nests with candle wax and matches stolen from his father's office.

Years later the world had spun. Vietnam became polarized after the French retreat. The CIA was forming opposition to the North as Ho Chi Minh began the organisation of infiltration into the South. In the States Jack Kennedy had become President, and shortly afterwards, as the American-backed attempt to overthrow Castro failed, the 'Bay of Pigs' crisis catapulted the planet towards Armageddon.

The family had stayed on in Vietnam, and Paul's father brought Americans to the house. Paul remembered them as being very big with short hair. They arrived in the early evening and were ushered quietly into his father's study. Paul was now old enough to meet them, in his teens, a dark mop of hair brushed across his forehead, as brown as the teak furniture.

'This is my son, Paul' his father said, as Paul moved forward and shook the large pink hand of the first American to enter his life.

'Good evening sir. How do you do?'

The big man smiled an easy smile. 'It's good that you speak English' he said.

'Yes sir, my father made sure of that!' smiled Paul.

'You speak Vietnamese as well I guess?'

'Yes sir, and French.'

'Hell boy, we could sure use someone like you! Your father here is doing a great job, but it ain't easy for us coming all the way over here trying to help sort your country out, I mean, sort Vietnam out, I guess your country's France.'

Paul hadn't really thought about his country as such. He had spent some time in France, and the Lycée in Saigon had been his bedrock of education. He loved Vietnam, but he wasn't sure how to answer. The big man answered for him.

'So Paul, I guess you're a free spirit then!'

Paul liked him, he liked his warmth, the way he smiled and treated him like an adult.

The American became a frequent visitor to the house over the months that followed, almost a family friend. He chatted to Paul endlessly about the States, his own home in North Carolina, how he had worked his way through college, what he thought America was trying to achieve in Vietnam.

'Hell Paul yuh know, a few years ago there were just seven hundred of us over here helping these people. Now there's more like seventeen thousand here, I dunno where it's going to end!'

Paul changed the subject.

'Sam, I'd really like to go to the States, and have a look round. I've almost finished here, you know, my baccalauréat. It's my last term and when that is over I will be free!' he grinned.

'Hell, you gotta talk to your father about that!'

'My Pa. He's been there hasn't he, to the States?' Paul was looking deep into Sam's blue eyes, probing, and he had learnt how to probe, to control his facial expressions and show no emotion, in the Asian way. He was also aware of his own charisma, his ability to charm and lead even this American agent, but Sam stared back, giving away less away than Paul had hoped for.

'I think that is something you should discuss with your father too', he said flatly.

'Oh, c'mon Sam! I know my father is working for the Americans, for you guys. I know the rubber plantation doesn't make us any money now, how has he paid for everything since the French had to leave?'

'Your Pa's been a huge help, he only wants what's best for this country and what's best for his family.'

'C'mon Sam, tell him to let me get over there, sure I could work and pay my way through college! You did it didn't you?!'

Sam laughed, caught in his own trap. 'You're smart alright, I'll talk to him for you.'

Paul was lucky. He spent the next three years in New Orleans as a student at Tulane. He was even luckier, he managed to rent a small apartment in the French quarter. He loved America. One summer he hitched from Louisiana into Mississippi through to Memphis and caught a Greyhound to Cincinnati. He went up to

Chicago and down to St Louis. Another time he went across to Houston, up to Dallas, Fort Worth and across to Alpaca. Another time he went to L.A. and then north up the coast to see the seals and the redwoods in the spring. Every other summer vacation he worked in construction, at weekends he doubled up as a waiter. Occasionally unexpected money appeared in his bank account, a letter would sometimes follow, from Vietnam. '... N'oublie jamais que tu es mon fils, tu me manques beaucoup. Papa.'

'... Don't ever forget that you are my son, I miss you very much. Papa.'

In his third year at Tulane he got an unexpected phone call from Sam, who said he was passing through and thought he'd drop in to 'see how you're doing'.

They met in the Quarter, in a bar off Lafayette.

'Strange town this. The Big Easy, I always travel well packed.' He opened his jacket to reveal a 9mm Colt automatic in an easily accessible holster.

'So Paul, how do you like it here then?'

'I really like it Sam. I like it a lot. I've been all over you know, California, up through the Carolinas. The East coast, you name it!'

'Bet you never been to Milwaukee boy!'

'No, but I did get up to Chicago, – thought it was great! Why Milwaukee?'

'Ah it's nothing really, my folks were there for a while then they moved down to Knoxville, they moved around a bit, and we ended up nearer Washington. Did you ever make it there?'

'Oh yeah, yeah I did as a matter of fact.'

'So, what do you think of this situation we now have in the old country Paul, it looks like we got ourselves in a big hole there, eh?'

Paul became a touch aggressive. 'A shithole! Westmoreland and Johnson aren't doing the right things and there's no way it's a popular war, or hadn't you noticed?'

'For sure. Nobody wants it, but we're in it!' Sam changed tack. 'Say, do you feel like a walk down by the docks, it's a while since I've seen the ole Mississippi roll by!'

'Sure.'

They walked through the Quarter to the French market, across the railway line, and stood on the slightly higher ground the other side, overlooking the river. Both were silent for a while, pretending to watch the gulls and one of the river boats that was pulling in to the jetty.

'So you been into the swamps then? Bit like some of the stuff back home eh?' started Sam.

'C'mon Sam, what is it you're really doing here? What do you want? Does my father know you're here – is he still working for you? He sends me money sometimes, but never really says what he is doing.'

Sam shuffled and looked awkward. 'Paul, it's about your father partly that I've come. There's some bad news. He was working for us, you know, over there, and he was caught out. I'm sorry son.'

Some tears welled in Paul's eyes, but he found himself saying 'does my mother know?'

'Yeah. She knew all along the work he was doing for us, she had mixed feelings about it, but she loved him and she hated the VC.'

'How did it happen?'

'We've been changing our policies over there to some extent. Like you said, the search and destroy missions aren't really working, you know, Kissinger has been scouting around for peace possibilities but we reckon our best chance is to play the VC at their own game. We had special Ops going in and out of the North, a lot of the shit's been starting up in Cambodia. Your father was picking up intelligence from some of our operatives very close to Charlie and someone must have talked. One night he was up in a village, and uh ...'

Paul turned away from Sam, away from the Mississippi, and looked back over into the French market and the Quarter beyond.

'Where's my mother?'

'Paris. She's being looked after.'

Paul started to walk in silence back across the railway line, across the broken rocks and weeds, to the square in front of the market. Sam walked with him in silence. They sat down at a round table outside one of the bars, Paul ordered some tea, Sam ordered bourbon.

'You know of course I must avenge my father's death' said Paul, as if emotionless. Sam knew him better, he wouldn't let much show.

'When you've finished at Tulane this year, why don't

you try working with us son. That's your best revenge, help us in the fight against these bastards!'

'I need more than that Sam. I need blood! Get me out there Sam, just get me out there.'

'Well, the best I can do is to put you in for selection. You'll have to make it up to Virginia, we can move things along faster from there. In the meantime, you could do worse than to get yourself fit, get in some training and some small arms practice at the local range. With your background there should be no problem, but I can't guarantee anything, you understand.'

Paul sipped his tea. 'Thanks Sam.'

Paul's selection was almost a fait accompli. Tri-lingual in Vietnamese, French and English, physically fit, with a high degree of self control, he made a good candidate.

In the days when the CIA had come up with such brainwaves as potions to make Castro's beard fall out, Paul's courses post selection were at times literally surreal. Although the Army had given up the idea of using LSD either as a combat-enhancing drug for its own troops or as a debilitator for the enemy, the CIA was still keen to evaluate its potential. While Tim Leary was preaching his message of 'turn on tune in and drop out', the Agency, slightly worried about fringe crackpots like him, was interested in the affects acid could have on the wrong person at the wrong time, or the right person at the right time, depending on who you were and how you looked at it. For them, a good dose of acid in Ho's tea might have done wonders for the war effort, conversely a good dose of acid in their own tea seemed to be making them jumpy, paranoid and beginning to believe that Leary wasn't so nuts after all.

Paul took his first trip having successfully passed selection before his first assignment. The acid was the same and as pure as that used by Leary in the early experiments sponsored by the government, before it got cut like all the drugs on all the streets in all the world. He wandered around the gardens of a large house near Langley, the smell of the antique furniture taking him back to the corridors of the white mansion outside Saigon. The rubber plants and the clear blue summer sky took him back further, to his childhood. He cried. In the exploding patterns in the dirt beneath his feet he saw order in chaos, chaos in order. In the grass he saw the dharma body, at night he saw the stars were matter, he was matter, but it didn't matter.

He came down twenty-four hours later, and at the debriefing said that he would need to 're-expose myself' to the chemical to be of any help. He got some more, over a period of a month he took it three or four times, usually in the grounds of the Agency's white mansion. He came to terms with the child that he was, felt more comfortable with his French/Asian blood, and in between trips rationalized that after all working for the Agency in South Vietnam was, for the time being at least, the fulfilment of Karma.

Observed by other Agents during his trips, they added little to his report at de-briefings. They concluded that 'LSD did little to increase the abilities of our personnel, it made them susceptible to uncontrollable laughter, moods of quiet depression and introspection whilst suffering long bouts of disorientation'. Quite. Paul was a convert.

He stole some of the tabs and on leave continued the 'experiments'. He took it in the desert, by the ocean, in the mountains, in the cities, the cafes and burger joints. When he went back to Washington for assignment, he wanted to go home, north of Saigon, and he got what he wanted.

His first tour lasted six months. Saigon had become a strange mix, even by Asian standards. Shops and stalls that sold fruit, chicken, fish paste, candles and a load of tinned goods from France, now overflowed with shaving foam, Hershey bars, stereos, fake fir, cornflakes and cans of beans. If it was in the PX it was out on the streets.

He went out to the white mansion of his childhood, the Americans were occupying it, a colonel was quartered there. He gave the colonel the agreed front – 'I'm a correspondent for the Tribune', he even got him to pose for a photograph, 'for everyone back home'. The smell of teak had been replaced by tobacco and sweat.

Paul felt that his new friends were invading his homeland. He loved the States, his father had died working for the Americans, but he thought what they were doing there wasn't right. Half French himself, he didn't feel total kinship with Vietnam either. He was an outsider. Perhaps Sam had spotted this, the Agency knew. He had wanted to use the Agency to avenge his father's death, but who was using who?

His initial mission was easy. Having visited his Vietnamese friends around Saigon, he was to go further in country, to the villages where many of them had relations, find out from them what their sympathies were, if they knew Charlie and from there piece together the jigsaw of the VC. The CIA wanted to know what their political structure was.

His mission was to penetrate the peasant population, to gather information and then return with the information, allowing the communist cadres to be slaughtered later. In the words of the Americans, the VC organisers, those involved in its network creating propaganda and money were 'neutralised'. They were blown away.

Paul knew from the beginning he would screw around with his brief. When he was deeper in country, when he saw VC neutralized because of his mission, he stopped it.

He had quickly realized that the South Vietnamese officials were only interested in working for themselves, promoting their own efficiency. They were robbing enormous amounts from the US, as well as taking bribes from captured VC suspects who were then able to buy back their freedom. In the villages the pro-American authorities were meant to fill out monthly quotas of VC killed, but they exaggerated this enormously so that the South Vietnamese Government and the CIA believed the programme as a whole was a huge success. As the intelligence reports of VC killed flooded back to Saigon and the Agency, the funds flooded in. The more they said they killed, the more money they got. Paul did what most of the South Vietnamese people were doing, he pocketed it. He bought gold, diamonds, jade, antiques and sometimes the freedom of girls in the Saigon brothels. They took the cash back to their families in the villages and bought rice from the VC.

In his mind Paul rationalized his father's death and his own subsequent involvement in the Agency as a way for his father to provide for him, from beyond the grave. And he provided for him well. Paul became rich. He needed a route to get his wealth out of Vietnam and into the West, a stash for when his Agency days were over, when the war in Asia was over.

His mother was in Paris. He thought he could arrange a de-briefing at the American Embassy there, possibly even with Sam. The way back would be a stop over in Bangkok, Delhi and then straight to France. He knew the Agency was active in Thailand, and he also knew that in the days of the French war the Vietminh had used Bangkok as a shopping centre. The war in Vietnam both then and now spilled over into Thailand. After business arrangements there, he would try and squeeze a few weeks R&R in India.

The Agency didn't want him to be replaced in country. From the numbers of VC killed to them the mission was a huge success, but it could continue for three or four weeks without Paul, and through Sam he was able to get agreement for him to head for France. After five days in Saigon he jumped on a Hercules taking the boys to R&R in Bangkok.

In some ways Bangkok reminded him of Saigon. Volkswagens, Peugeots and 2 CVs mixed with Tuk Tuks and samlors. A lot of GIs were spilling out onto the streets, drinking beer and laughing with the Thai girls. Like Saigon, the heat was unforgiving. There was more of a bustle to the city, and the overcrowding made the heat fiercer. Everybody seemed to have a transistor radio, but unlike Vietnam it wasn't AFRS, Radio Saigon, belting out Motown, but the delicate sounds of traditional Thai music at full volume through cracked plastic.

He had Bangkok marked as a place for his future. He would cautiously bring some of his gems to the market, the Thai passion for precious stones was no less than anywhere else in the Far East, and the price of gold was rising. He had managed to buy both at good prices in Vietnam and would use Bangkok as a trading post, switching in and out of western currency as and when he needed it, before going back in to 'Nam and building up his reserves. He reckoned the war would last for years, by which time his wealth would be phenomenal. He would need help in retaining the empire he was going to build, whilst some of his recruits would undoubtedly be from the East, he thought that some contacts in the West would be useful. Some of the disillusioned students that he had met in the States perhaps. He would worry what to do with his empire when he had built it. One miracle at a time. The empire building gave him something to do, it gave him an objective away from the war, away from the meaningless mess of it all.

Like many visitors to Bangkok then and since he wandered along by the side of the Chaophraya River, looked round the Royal Palace and the Wat Phra Keo. Unlike many visitors to Bangkok, he used a C.I.A. contact from the American Embassy to meet with some of the wealthier Thais, and over beer, Mekhong whisky and kap klaem, began to discuss prices for some of his gems and bullion.

They spoke in English. Paul was cautious, the Thais thought he had probably stolen the gold from the Americans and was selling it onto them cheap. True. The gems were even more delicate, but greed prevailed. For the Thais to get word back to anyone in the Embassy about their discussions would have meant the deals would have to stop, and as far as the Thais were concerned, they were only just beginning. Paul though had decided to use these particular contacts just the once, get hold of some of the dollars he badly wanted, and then return to Bangkok next R&R to spend some time rooting out fresh contacts himself. He figured that if, in the meantime, things did go wrong and word got back somehow to the Agency, the amounts he would sell this time were small enough not to cause too much of a stir. Also, he thought, the Agency itself was funding some of the programme, possibly by drug dealing, and they would not want this to come out.

Paul had been brought up with opium, it was used

by some of the workers on the plantation and he had tried it at quite an early age. It wasn't really his thing, he thought he might save it for his old age. Heroin was a 'different kettle of poissons', as his father would say. The end result was the same, but whilst opium was like a winding trail, H was the motorway.

By this time Paul had become cynical enough not to expect any government anywhere to do what it said it would do, or to have any morals, and it was no surprise to him that the President was a major player in some very unpleasant deals. He didn't buy the theory that this President didn't know what the Agency was up to, and there had been some disquieting rumblings about its involvement in the Kennedy assassination. There had been further rumblings about his predecessor's involvement in the neutralization of one Marilyn Monroe. Paul preferred to deal with the VC, he knew where he was.

The deal with the Thais was closed, Paul had his dollars. He spent the day relaxing, preparing for his flight to India which left at 11.00 a.m. the next morning, to a continent which had never considered the men of the sword or the possession of money as superior. As the Indian poet said:-

The East bowed low before the blast
In patient, deep disdain;
She let the legions thunder past
And plunged in thought again.

✳

'You see my friend our inner elements, forces and functions can be separate, they can dissolve, then they can combine and set new and formally impossible forces to work; they can be transformed by internal processes.' Paul saw the exploding patterns breaking up, reforming, the dharma body in the grass.

He stared into the dark brown eyes of the old man, a warm breeze blew across from the ocean. The old man was still talking about the Vedanta. He smiled, then changed the subject.

'We too had our colonies in Cambodia. India is the mother of all Asia.'

They were north of Delhi, up in the hills, in Menali, which had some of the best dope in India. Paul liked to get stoned. Menali was high in a valley which he reached by risking his life at the hands of a suicidal Sikh bus driver. Menali was a strange kind of Shangrila. He stayed in a wooden house built on posts with a rickety staircase running up through the middle, a stream trickled down the mountain behind his bedroom. The stream was everybody's bathroom, and Paul was glad he wasn't in the village below. He spent ten days there, walking, visiting people in the village, smoking, watching the sun set. He had met the old man on his way back down to catch the Sikh's suicide run to Delhi.

At first he found India enervating, the low standard of living, the high rate of dying. On one hand life was empty, ugly and shoddy, surrounded by the horrors of poverty. On the other hand his chance meeting with the old man had allowed him to glance at the roots of the East, to begin to understand the branches on the Asian tree.

'The river flows continuously and appears to be the same from moment to moment, yet the waters are forever changing.'

Paul looked up. 'It's time I was going.' He thought of the Mekong. He thought, 'if you sit by the river long enough, the bodies of your enemies will drift past you.'

The old man knew what he was thinking. Paul knew he knew. He left in silence.

Twenty-four hours later he arrived at Orly in Paris. Sam met him at the airport, it was cold and raining. He was glad that his splashdown in the West was happening in France, his father's home.

'Long time no see!' grinned Sam.

'Yeah. How's my mother?' The question caught Sam slightly off guard, Paul had guessed that his mother and Sam had become more than just friends.

'She misses her son.'

'Touché!' Paul still liked him, but he was a danger now.

'You've got a day to recover then it's debriefing at 0900 hours, you know where.'

In Paris the Agency used the Embassy for most of its work, although both Sam and Paul had sniggered in the past at some of its clichéd fronts, the last one a brothel in Pigalle.

Paul was tired, shattered and spaced out. He thought

his debriefing would be easy, based on the reports already sent and his unique experience in the field which, as far as he knew, only he could substantiate. He would have known had there been another operative watching.

They got into a Peugeot 404 diesel cab, and Sam got down to business.

'Before you go back we want you to visit another director who's not too well. He's over near London, and thinks he could improve business there. He's in admin, and is short of sales staff. Does that appeal to you?'

'Why not?' Paul had thought of recruits from the disaffected students at Tulane, he knew about the anti-war marches in London, a lot of Americans were travelling around there and he might even find someone British to help with his empire building. The older Brits he had met seemed devious, always understating everything, but the younger ones were just like the kids in America.

'How long would they need help for do you think?'

'Probably three to six months.'

'And what about business elsewhere?'

'Well depending on what you say over the next two or three days, we figure it's sufficiently well set up for our local reps to continue without management input. You could be contacted once when and if it's necessary, if it starts to slide then we'll have to re-think things. Obviously we have one or two other managers who will be able to dep. for you but we know ultimately the local reps will respond best to you. Have a think about it, let me know over the next few days.'

The two day debrief was hard. Sam played it by the book, it was formal, involving two other operatives Paul hadn't met before. It unnerved him, but only slightly. Sam and the other two Agents were possibly more unnerved by Paul. He had a way, an ability to turn the tables, where the questioner became the questioned.

'Tell me about our rep in London. I need a change from little men in black pyjamas.' He stared at Sam who looked down.

'You know we've tried to persuade our friends there to help us in 'Nam. That bastard Wilson talked them out of it but we're hoping a conservative government might change the picture. We have been applying pressure on some particular ministers and all the indications are that if we were able to help the party funds then the party would be able, in due course, to help us in our efforts. Specifically one or two cabinet ministers could be open to persuasion and our representative would need help in ensuring that these ministers made the right decision.'

Paul smiled. He guessed what was coming.

'What that guy Profumo was up to is nothing compared to some of these guys. With a little help we can get the backing in their cabinet and we feel that a NATO presence in your old country would do a great deal to quiet things down at home and provide us with some relief. As you know, this is the only war the Brits have stayed out of. We need to endorse, to bolster up the special relationship.'

Paul nodded. It reminded him of the Castro sagas, but provided he was able to keep his openings back in Saigon, he welcomed the opportunity to recruit some help for himself, and he'd never been to England.

The Meeting

*P*AUL'S ARRIVAL in the U.K. was uneventful. From the Embassy in Mayfair he went further west to meet his connection around Bayswater.

The Agency had short-listed three ministers who might be susceptible to pressure, because of financial and marital problems. One liked to gamble, and more than one had been repetitively unfaithful to his wife and could be open to the overtures of a glamourous call-girl. Numerous venues which were already wired were available, but it was the delicate matter of setting up an ally that had led to deliberations within the CIA. The English public were touchy about the U.S. nuclear bases, the mutually hushed-up catastrophe at Greenham Common in the late 1950's had made both governments cautious and any scandal would fuel the growing anti-war movement.

Paul toyed with the idea of carefully leaking the Agency's plans, exposing any honey trap to MI5, and embarrassing the Americans. Thinking it through, he thought that even if two or three British ministers put pressure on the government to support America in Vietnam, it would come to nothing. He doubted that troops would be sent. He felt that the Brits would have handled Vietnam differently, more along the SAS 'hearts and minds' campaign in Borneo. They also had their own war in Oman, about which the British public knew nothing. He decided to play ball with his brief, hoping to get some time out in England, and further his own moves.

After three weeks the CIA came up with two proposals for two different ministers. One honey trap, one financial embarrassment leading to bankruptcy unless the victim was propped up by additional funding, from the Agency. His boss agreed he should stay around for the initial stages of each to be put into place, to see how they worked and whether or not, in the event of failure, they would need to come up with something else. They gave it six to eight weeks, and for a month or so Paul could lay low in the U.K.

Notting Hill was a short distance from Bayswater and he began to hang out there. He liked it. He also realised that the disaffection among the young with their government, the war in Asia, the Cold War and fear of nuclear holocaust would provide him with plenty of recruits for his empire. He might even tell them about the secret war their own government was running in Oman.

His time at Tulane hadn't been wasted. He had consumed America thirstily, and examined carefully the chalice from which he drank. The American aboriginal peoples had shared a humility with those in the East, of which the immigrants had lost sight. It was this loss of contact with the earth, the push to control the world around them which he felt had led the Americans astray, had led them to Vietnam.

He studied the Old World of the British Celts, driven to the west of the islands, to Cornwall, Wales, Ireland and America. He had already promised himself if he ever made it back to the Old World, a trip to the western part of Britain was a must. He read that Cornwall was full of standing stones, aligned stone circles and other megalithic monuments. The alignments reminded him of the dragon paths in Vietnam. He found out that the Celtic pagans believed in chakras, the energy routes passing through the body. They were used by the witches of old Britain, who had a base chakra coloured red through to the violet crown chakra. Near Delhi the old man had told him about 'Kundalini' and the chakras. What was it doing here, in pagan Britain, two thousand years ago? He discovered the British fascination for ghosts. In the east, ghosts and spirits of the dead were looked upon more generally as friendly forces, he found it strange that in the west they were feared. Was it to allow the most famous ghost of all, Jesus, to keep his position as King of ghosts? For Paul the summoning of spirits of the ancestors was normal, but the west had a huge lack of acceptance of the power of the mind. It was only recently, in the early 1960's, they had given a word to part of it – psychokinesis – the ability to move objects by the power of the mind alone. The same was true of their views on rein-carnation, healing powers, travelling out of the body, dreaming, precognition and other activities which in the east were generally accepted. It didn't bode well for the west, and without renewed understanding, or a new understanding, Paul felt it was on a path to self-destruction. It was 1969, it was time for a new age to begin.

He thought that his recruits ought to be not only able to work with him back in Vietnam, but should have some idea of what they would try and achieve once they had got enough wealth to give them some power. He would need to introduce them into the ways of their own past, the ways which connected with the East; he didn't expect his task to be very difficult, a lot of the young understood all was not well on planet earth.

He headed west, to Cornwall, only weeks after Steve had met Mike in Notting Hill before leaving in the same direction. Paul met them on a beach as the sun was setting. He had been sitting, watching the sunset as they came out of the surf looking the same at first glance, blonde and tanned. Paul looked up. 'Good waves?'

'Yeah, pretty good – a good swell coming in, especially for this time of year!'

An American, perfect. He looked at the other one, less sure of himself.

'I'm still learning.'

He smiled, he was open, earnest, powerfully built.

'He's gonna be really good! He's a natural, goofy, but

such a natural!' said the American.

Paul put Steve somewhere from the Mid-West, Colorado may be.

'Where are you from then?' asked the American.

Paul paused. 'Well, my mother's Indian and my father was French.'

'Wow, that's a strange combination!'

The English guy blurted it out, and now looked slightly embarrassed.

'Actually, I've just come back from India. I've got some nice Kashmir twists with me, do you want to smoke a joint?'

'You've been to India – you brought some dope back with you, from Kashmir?'

It couldn't have been easier. The surfers had an old VW camper parked up nearby, their gear was in it, surf mags, a book on *Walden Pond* by Thoreau, crash bags, surf wax, wet suits, some old surfing photos stuck to the inside and a large picture of Hendrix. Paul took a huge toke on the conical joint he had just rolled and passed it onto the American. He took a huge drag, his eyes fixed on the picture of Hendrix as he did so.

'Pity we can't get a stereo to go in here!'

'They've got those eight track things, but they're so crap and so expensive. Imagine, soon people will be able to sit in their vans getting stoked with some kind of incredible sound system going as they look out over the sunset. Wouldn't that be great!'

Their idea of nirvana obviously had some way to go, but then Paul had some time. Steve passed the joint on to Mike, Paul rolled another one.

'We've gotta bit of grass' said Mike. 'Would you like to try some?'

'Yeah. I'll tell you what, we'll make a cocktail, we'll mix it up with this Kashmiri, just smoke the grass and the dope. I don't like mixing tobacco with it, I don't suppose you do much either?' he said looking at Steve.

'Well, I guess not too much, I like to smoke it straight.'

'Have you ever dropped acid?' said Paul. He eyeballed them both as he said it.

'No' said Mike. 'It's pretty heavy isn't it, I mean it's screwed some people up.'

'Yeah, well it can do. You've gotta feel for yourself whether it's right for you. Do you feel it's right?'

'I really can't say, I suppose if the place and the time felt okay ...'

The following three or four days they hung out together. While Steve and Mike were surfing, Paul read or sat gazing out across the ocean. He read a book every two days, his current title was *Apparitions* by G Tyrrell. A ghost book.

One Hand Ian pitched up, Paul said he had met him hanging around Notting Hill and had dropped him a postcard with the name of the village they were in, giving their address as the beach. Ian had brought some more books down for Paul. *The Search for Bridey Murphy*, *The Man and Time* by J B Priestley, an old edition of the *Tibetan Book of the Dead*.

Mike and Steve tried not to look as One Hand Ian rolled a joint with one hand, he produced a floppy but smokable mixture of Paul's Kashmir and Steve's grass with some rolling tobacco thrown in.

The summer was slowly fading, the nights were drawing in. Paul slept in the van, the others still slept on the beach. One Hand Ian never seemed to close his eyes; Steve used to look at him sometimes as he woke in the night, and Ian would be there, his back propped up against the tyre of the van, staring out into space. One night he caught Steve looking at him, and Steve felt uncomfortable, as if Ian was vibing him to go back to sleep. He did. He had dreams of blue-green hills, covered by fog and mist which hung like a wet sheet over the body of the earth. People were walking round the hills, a donkey train loaded with guns. They were small, dark people in black pyjamas. He joined them on their trail down from the mountain, into the forest and suddenly, out of the mist, they came across a temple of crumbling red bricks. Large plants reached in through the doors and small windows, searching in the dark. At the far end of the temple sat a large golden Buddha. Steve woke. As usual, One Hand Ian sat staring, this time at the ground about three feet in front of him. 'Go back to sleep.' Steve returned to sleep, he dreamed of a huge swell, of riding massive waves as if he were being guided across them.

'Surf's up!' It was Mike. Six a.m., the sun had probed the mist enough for them to see a small three to four foot swell delivering perfect waves on the long blue beach. Mike got out of his crash bag, and into his wetsuit which was still damp and cold. They made off to

109

the surf, automatically eyeing up the waves to watch for a lull to paddle out, the breeze was offshore, the water was clear but chilly.

As they came in from the surf Paul had made some tea, they wolfed down bread, fruit and yoghurt. One Hand Ian never seemed to eat, he sipped his tea, putting it down in the sand between sips as he rolled another joint.

'I've been looking in the local newspaper here,' said Paul. 'Do you know, you can rent one of these small cottages for next to nothing in the winter. I wouldn't mind doing that – I'll have to be away for quite some time but I could put up for the rent or most of it and if you two wanted to we could share the place. You could surf through the winter then!'

And that's how they came to live in the cottage on the moor. After the seance, a month or so later, Paul went up to London to meet with his connection and a de-brief at the Embassy. From there he returned to Vietnam. A honey trap had worked and pressure was placed on the cabinet to intervene in the Vietnam war, but it came to nothing. Harold Wilson was no fool in that regard.

Paul's task was done. He expected that from an R&R in Bangkok he would be able to summon Mike and Steve, meet them in India, take them up to Delhi to meet the old man, the guru, and from there begin to unveil some of the plans he had laid. He would enjoy playing Mephistopheles again.

Consequently he knew nothing about the accident

after the seance. He knew nothing about Mike's acid trip, and nothing of his death.

Back in theatre he continued with his part in the Phoenix Operation. The body counts became more and more exaggerated, the funding grew and Paul had to get out to Bangkok to buy into his future. It wasn't hard for him to make his own contacts and he was also able to meet a Parisian lawyer who introduced him to the offshore world, how to fund and set up companies which he could control for direct investments into the States or Europe.

He sneaked a week in Paris, and there laid plans with two-ex advisors to the Bank of America who were helpful in explaining to him how to set up and fund these investments. A company would be set up with Paul as the sole shareholder and managing director allowing him access to corporate America. This was on the tax planning side, it was legitimate and encouraged by other corporate advisors. Real estate or shares could be purchased in the name of the companies, the source of the funding was not questioned, and the IRS were often hard pushed to get their percentage. Paul reflected for a moment on that, on giving the Government back a proportion of its gift to him. He decided they would only waste it.

From Paris he sent a postcard to Steve and Mike, suggesting that they should meet him as he had some "interesting news". The card arrived at the cottage but by this time Mike was dead. Steve had left and was off with Kate, haunted by his dreams, hexes, magic and

Paul. Paul went back from Paris to Vietnam. Six weeks later he contrived an excuse to go to Bangkok and hitched what was by now his habitual ride on a Hercules C130. It took off in the early morning mist, circling above the blue hills before heading west to Thailand.

At around the same time Steve was sitting on a Jumbo Jet which had left Heathrow airport heading east.

In The Temple
of the
Golden Buddha

*B*USINESS FOR PAUL in Bangkok was not difficult. He had a product that the Thais wanted and he could afford to sell it at an attractive price. In financial terms his cost base was zero. In those days the dollar was still the currency to be in, and he had a lot of it. He spread deposits throughout the banks in Bangkok, changed a considerable amount into baht and set off for the hills of northern Thailand.

When Steve arrived in Chiang Mai the air was cool and fresh, a blue mist hung over the distant hills, he was struck by the calmness of the town compared to the furore of Bangkok. He walked for a while, getting used to the Thai set-up of places to stay. Compared to Bangkok he felt he was going back in time. As he walked into town he saw girls in brightly coloured tunics with yellow skin and dark brown eyes. He'd read up what he could, and realized they were girls from the hill tribes of the Karen who had come into town to market. He wanted to get out into the hills and had heard that travellers would sometimes team up together in a group of three or four to go up north of the Kok river. There weren't many westerners around as he walked along the Tapae road looking for somewhere to stay. He had no idea that a few years later the Thais would set up small trekking companies to help the adventurous like himself, and that a few years after that the place would be over-trekked.

He thought of Mike as he walked, of Kate, of home, the States. Vietnam in relative terms was just around the corner. He guessed the people wouldn't be so different to these, that the small towns would be like this, but beneath the waves of B52's. He wondered about Paul, ghosts, his hand ran over the small leather-bound prayer book Father Wallace had given him.

Unlike Bangkok there were very few places to stay in Chiang Mai. He managed to find a small family run guest house, it opened mainly in February for the flower festival, but they seemed happy to put him up in a small room with a bed and a light. No shower, no fan. He didn't care. He wasn't tired, he went out in the early morning air as the yellow fingers of the sun began to probe the shadows.

Paul had arrived two days earlier, he had walked out of the station in the same direction as Steve, over the river, along the Ta Pae road and then turned left, finding himself a place to stay west of the river. Now he was thinking of going east from Chiang Mai, to try and relieve the Agency of some funds which it was gathering at an alarming rate from covert operations in Laos. In his mind Paul called it 'the white circle', white into

116

gold. Smack into dollars. Smoking a bit of O was one thing, scamming large amounts of smack was something else. He couldn't believe that even the Agency was doing that. For the time being he decided to stay in Chiang Mai, perhaps go out and try to visit one or two of the hill tribes. They were migrants from Tibet, China and Laos who didn't care about countries. Quite a few came from Burma, and apparently one, the Mienthi, came from central China. The women wore black jackets and trousers.

A dog snapped at Paul's heels, he turned and looked up into the face of a tall westerner. Paul knew he was American, he guessed ex GI, AWOL at the very least.

'Hi' said Paul.

'Ah you speak English?' said the American.

'Yeah' As usual the farang had mistaken Paul for a Thai.

'Yeah. I learned it off one of you guys.' Well at least it wasn't a lie.

'Great. I've been here a while now and it sure is hard to make yourself understood sometimes!'

'Well yeah. It's the same for me actually. I'm not Thai, I'm mainly Vietnamese.' Paul paused to let it sink in. The blinds were lifted from the American's eyes, a deserter for sure. 'So uh, is there anywhere around here you can get a cool drink?' asked Paul.

'Sure, yeah there's a place just down the road. I'm staying there, been there for a while now, since, since I came here.'

'Nice place, Chiang Mai, nice and laid back eh? A guy

could forget a lot here, just lay back and watch the war go by.'

'The war, yeah. Guess that must have had a real effect on you, eh, I mean being Vietnamese and all?'

'Well, yeah. I lost my Pa because of it.'

'Gee, I'm sorry.'

That's okay, thought Paul, guilt by association would make his new friend more compliant.

Steve began to notice the quiet almost hidden hustle of Chiang Mai. It was, after all, a trading town, not too far from Burma and Laos. The smuggling in teak and gems, the trading in guns and narcotics were all part of the fabric of the villages and towns just a stone's throw away. He wanted to get out to them and up towards the northern borders, crossing the Mekong. The river flowed so far, here through valleys of peace where the only disturbance was the occasional squabbling between the opium growers and the war lords who controlled the crops. A long way from the Mekong Delta. He thought he would head out of town, get on a bus and go from village to village, see where the trail took him. He was adrift.

He had his backpack on, and was walking in a northerly direction, half looking for a bus, half deciding to walk until he was too tired to walk anymore when he would try and find a safe place to crash. Some Thais were squatting by the side of the road, looking in a southerly direction, over his shoulder. He turned and looked. A bus was coming up the road and he jumped on it.

It was crowded. A young Thai boy and another older Thai were trying to usher chickens from the rear up towards the front, and as the bus jolted off down the road the chickens flapped above the heads of the passengers. All the seats were taken, Steve stood at the back with several Thais. Three kilometres or so up the road the bus stopped. Nobody got off, but several more people got on. The aisle between the seats was jammed, he was squashed up against the rear window. It seemed that the bus was now going in the wrong direction. He wanted to head north, but the bus was going south. He had a map on him and looked up the next town that he thought the bus would pass through, Ngao, and said this to one of the Thais next to him. The Thai smiled pleasantly, nodded his head and agreed.

'Ngao'.

Steve then pointed in the northern direction towards Ngao.

'Ngao?'.

'Ngao' said the Thai, smiling. Confusing.

For reasons known only to themselves the bus company ran the bus south to Lampang before turning ninety degrees and heading north up to Chiangrai through Ngao. It stopped frequently and from time to time the driver went round and collected fares from people who didn't already have tickets. Steve thought he would stay until the end of the line, not realizing that this would take close to nine hours.

Paul changed his mind, he wouldn't go east, he would go north.

'So have you been out of Chiang Mai, up into the triangle?'

'Sure, had to go and have a look at the Mekong, yuh know, with all that shit going on around the Delta and ...'

So, thought Paul, a deserter, or was he?

'How long have you been in Thailand then?' He was subject to Paul's piercing stare.

'Oh, a few months now. I came over, just travelling around, you know. I thought of going to 'Nam, take some pictures, you know, try and sell 'em, but I didn't fancy getting shot at by no Gook! Oh shit, I'm sorry, I didn't mean, I mean ...'

'That's okay, I'm only half Gook,' said Paul.

The deserter continued. 'Look, hey I've got some contacts up near Chiansen, it's just up past Chiangrai. You know you can have a great time there. There's some beautiful girls, dope, you know, you can really kick back man.'

Paul had done his homework. He knew that Chiangsaen housed the ruins of many temples, and ramparts from earlier kingdoms which were still intact. Looking for them would be good enough cover. It was also in Chiangsaen that the Agency had an operative, and it was already on his itinerary.

'I know a guy who goes up there, he's got an old truck and we could hitch a ride if you like. If you take the bus it takes hours, but this guy will take us straight up there, maybe with a stopover for a bite. Interested?'

The American looked slyly at Paul. 'Sure. When?'

'Well, he usually goes up about mid-week, which I reckon is sometime around now. Say we meet up here for breakfast round 8.30 a.m. and then we'll wander on up, see what my friend's doing. I guess you speak Thai?'

Of course, thought Paul, and two dialects of Chinese.

'No, but I'm sure we'll get by' he smiled, 'I'm gonna go get some rest and write a few letters. See you here in the morning. By the way, my name is Paul.'

'Hi, I'm Rick!'

The bus station in Chiangrai was a short walk from the centre of town. The town faced onto the Maekok river and lacked the charisma of Chiangmai. For different reasons Steve, like Paul, had done his homework and would use the town as a base, either to trek from or, more probably, to carry on to somewhere else. He found somewhere to stay by making his now almost familiar walk towards the river. He ate some food from one of the roadside stalls and, exhausted from his trip, went to sleep.

The owner of the guest house he was staying in spoke a few words of English, and told Steve about the ruins at Chiangsaen. Steve bought into the idea and took the owner's advice, sharing a taxi to the town which was about an hour away. He wasn't disappointed. It was a one-street town on the banks of the Mekong. He liked it, he felt as if he had arrived at his destination. This time though his walk towards the river produced nowhere to stay. There didn't seem to be anywhere. He felt safe, he thought he might sleep out of town, walk into the country and find shelter in one of the ruins. There were a lot of monks in town in saffron robes, walking quietly with their begging bowls, some serious, some smiling and talking to each other. They were walking in a northerly direction and although hungry, Steve began to follow them.

It was early evening, the road was dusty but somehow he felt fresh and awake. There was a scent in the air of spring flowers, although spring was long past. The monks walked in silence, setting the pace with determination, and he struggled to keep up. Two of the monks at the rear of the party slowed down, and turned towards Steve. He continued walking, smiled and bowed as he approached them. They returned the greeting. He walked along with them and the walking became easier. His feet felt light and he no longer felt hungry.

The monks led him along simple tracks, up into the hills, across streams and a small river crossing where there was a bamboo bridge. At last they arrived at a collection of tropical bungalows, set in a clearing amongst the forest. Petals of white flowers were strewn across the floors of all of them, some children were playing with goats, chickens roamed and a small pack of dogs scampered around. At the bungalows the monks split off in different directions, Steve was left with the monk who had been at the front. He beckoned him up the steps of one of the bungalows. Removing their shoes they went inside.

'You Englishman?' said the monk.

Steve was slightly taken back. 'No, I'm American.'

'Ah, American.' said the monk, smiling.

Steve began to wish he'd said English. Blood flowed into the Mekong, the river whispered its secrets to the monks; secrets of young men killed in foreign parts who had no reason to be there, of other young men, in black cotton uniforms and conical hats who fought to defend their mothers, sisters and wives from the invader.

'Tea?' said the monk.

Steve smiled. 'Thank you. Where did you learn to speak English?'

'I speak very badly. Some Americans came here sometime ago. They were tired and hungry and they needed peace and rest. They taught me to speak your language.'

Steve was puzzled.

'They have gone now, they do not come any more.' said the monk.

The bungalow smelt of magnolia blossom. The sun warmed Steve's back as he sat cross-legged opposite the monk who poured the tea from a clay pot. They sat in silence for some time.

'Would you like to see our temple? We call it wat. Temple, that is right?'

Steve smiled. 'Yes, temple, yes please.' He followed the monk out of the bungalow along a small path which led out of the settlement and up into the hills. They toiled for some twenty minutes as the incline grew steeper until they reached a small plateau which had been cleared, overlooking the monks' settlement and the river nearby. On the plateau was a temple which Steve thought he had seen already somewhere.

They walked in silence to the steps and went in between two stone pillars, across the floor where the monk bowed and prayed. Steve waited until he had finished, and then they walked together towards a Buddha. It sat cross-legged some eight feet high, gleaming in the dark, as it must have gleamed for thousands of years. The monk turned.

'This is the brother of the Golden Buddha in Wat Traimit. Like that Buddha, it is Sukhothai. It was covered and hidden here, hundreds of years ago when the Burmese came and Thailand was invaded. It is a secret, we know you had to come here, and we know that when you leave our secret will be safe.'

Everything the monk said was true. Steve realised also that he was completely and utterly lost, that when he followed the monks from town, he had no recollection of how long it took them to arrive at the monastery, even by which direction they had travelled.

They went back to the monastery and the monk spoke again.

'You will be tired, you will need to rest. Please eat the evening meal with us and tomorrow you must tell me about your journey.'

It was 9.15 a.m., the sun was already warm and the streets of Chiangmai had been busy for several hours. The night market had transformed peacefully to the commerce of the morning. True to his word the deserter's friend turned up with his truck and was happy to take them up to Chiangsaen. The deserter's friend, a Thai, was called Master Joe.

'Why Master Joe?' asked Paul.

'He used to teach Muay Thai, trouble is, he found he liked the old whisky more than the boxing, and his pupils kind of dried up!' laughed Rick, not really answering the question. Then he added 'He's a master of Muay Thai.'

Master Joe glared at him. He was small to the point of looking fragile, about five feet two, possibly five three, at the most. Paul found it hard to imagine that he was not only a master of the ancient Thai martial art but had apparently been a champion of twenty-one bouts of which he'd won nineteen and drawn two. Of the nineteen he won, eleven were by straight knock-out. This was apparently from the flying knee technique which was perfected by Master Joe and used with extraordinary ruthlessness. He was also deemed to be an expert with his elbows.

'I suppose whisky and martial arts is a lethal combination' said Paul somewhat flatly. He sensed that Master Joe didn't like him, but he guessed also that Master Joe probably didn't like anybody.

The truck bounced over the dirt road and Rick and Master Joe lit cigarettes, Camels. Dust seemed to get into the cabin of the truck through every nook and cranny and the combination of the Camels and the dust made breathing an interesting exercise. After half an hour or so Master Joe pulled out a bottle of Hongyok whisky, took a swig and offered it to Rick who took a swig and passed it on to Paul. It was one of the cheaper brands of rice whisky and left you with a truck-sized hangover. Rick took another gulp as he passed it back to Master Joe, who took several more large swigs and kept the bottle in his right hand as he wiped his mouth and nose with the back of his left hand. The truck veered to the left following the vague camber of the track, and Master Joe casually righted it with his left hand, hanging on to the Hongyok.

Why Joe? The Master bit was clear enough, but why Joe.

'Why Joe?' Paul expected Rick to answer, but enlivened by his hit of whisky, Master Joe answered for himself.

'My name is Narong. Farangs find it easier to remember Joe. I went to the States for a couple of years, tried to teach them Muay Thai. They don't understand anything, so I come back here, but I keep my name, Master Joe.'

He took another hit of Hongyok. 'I suppose it's all Kung fu and karate over there?' said Paul.

'Stupid karate! You learn Muay Thai with me in three months you beat black belt easy. Stupid Chinese! Stupid Kung fu!'

'Maybe the States isn't ready for Muay Thai yet' said Paul.

'Americans want everything quick. They lazy, don't want to work.'

'Hell man. Take it easy!' said Rick.

Master Joe had veered off the track and they were hurtling along a narrow footpath leading to one of the villages by the roadside.

'We'll stop here, get some coffee' said Master Joe, obstinately driving on the footpath until they reached the village.

Paul liked him. Having seen some of the Thai boxers in action he tended to agree with Master Joe's analogy, the Thai martial art was probably superior to any other form on a one to one basis. Still, what few people didn't mention was that by the age of twenty-one or twenty-two the Thai boxer was at his peak, and unlike the Chinese or Japanese martial artists, few of the boxers went onto study more. There was more, but only one or two who had graced the big stadiums in Bangkok or the smaller rings in the country fairs would ever learn all the secrets of their martial art. Master Joe was a Bangkok cocktail, wrapped tight and ready to explode at any moment.

They couldn't find anywhere to get coffee and made do with green tea. Back in the truck Master Joe carried on with the whisky, and conversation was all but impossible because of the noise, the dust, and his style of driving which threw the two passengers around as he bumped on and off the track. They both thought it better not to comment.

At Chiangsaen though, Master Joe opened up the conversation over another pot of green tea.

'It's near here there is famous golden Buddha, hidden by monks in forest.'

The ramblings of a drunk? Or the thread of truth picked up around the country boxing circuits where perhaps a Master of Muay Thai was the brother or relation of a monk? In any case Paul wanted to dump his travelling companions. Having got close to his destination, he needed to winkle out the Agency's operative in Chiangsaen, check the story of the Buddha, the dope scamming and everything else. Paul got up and left Rick and Master Joe pulling the stopper from a second bottle of Hongyok. They were both too far gone to know or care what he was up to and he faded away quietly into the shadows.

He found his contact eating some noodle soup with a side dish of morning glory vine fried in garlic. Paul was hungry and ordered the same noodles fried with vegetables, egg and peanuts. His contact looked tired with dark rings beneath his eyes, sunken cheeks and a general aura of poor health. Paul pegged him as untrustworthy, out for himself, somewhat like me, he thought wryly. Still he was a different kettle of poissons to Paul, Paul was building something, this guy was all but finished. He called himself Lee. They talked about basic Agency business, whether the NVA were building up to the extent it had been rumoured, how the CIA was using its influence outside theatre in countries like Thailand, the local scene in Chiangsaen. Lee had been across the border and several hundred kilometres into Laos and North Vietnam. From there he had gone down in to South Vietnam before hopping on one of the R&R C130's back to Bangkok and up to the north again. He didn't give much away, the question of alleged drug dealing by the Agency was never broached. They agreed to meet the next day, and so it went on for four days until Lee asked him if he wanted to smoke some O. Paul said he'd be delighted and in the afternoon went to a small private house which was expensively furnished.

The house had a faint smell of the old plantation about it, Paul thought of his mother and father. His quest for revenge was buried but not dead. They went through the entrance porch into a hallway through an arch, down some steps into a pleasant room where the sunlight filtered through the blinds and plants against the window. Inside a well dressed young Thai with a chubby face and long hair smiled and ushered them in past a table placed between two chaises-longues. The young Thai spoke to Paul's contact in Thai, and he translated for Paul.

'He says welcome to his house, he's sorry that he doesn't speak any of your languages, but would you please make yourself at home ...' The young Thai interrupted, 'he says he has prepared a pipe for us each and he will send in his boy to attend us.'

Paul nodded his head and smiled.

The opium explained his contact's lacklustre appearance. For Paul the smoke was a means to an end. Opium didn't affect him in the same way as it affected most other people. He found that although it relaxed him, it gave him a lot of physical energy and the opium bed for him was a mite tedious. His new-found friend on the other hand was clearly at home. He smoked two pipes more or less straight off, lay back on the bed and crashed out.

Paul's mind wandered back to his childhood, to the large American with pink hands, the ants nests he used to blow up with the matches stolen from his father's study. He saw these images very clearly, as if watching himself in a movie. They mingled with other images, with a river that flowed like a black vein through the body of Asia. All his secrets began and ended there. In its waters Paul swam to a chamber of golden sunlight. In the chamber a naked Indian woman sat with a snake coiled around her. Behind her lay the beaches of southern California, the palms rustled gently in the breeze, he could smell the surf and hear the waves breaking. He walked towards the woman who changed into the old man he had met north of Delhi. The old man smiled and with his hand ushered him towards the beach. As he stepped onto the beach it changed into the dark mud beneath the surface of the river, the water swayed and undulated, he walked between the plants on the river bed. The ground grew steeper, he was walking up a hill to where the water grew lighter, shafts of sunlight stood before him like golden pillars where millions of small dust like particles danced. As he walked he grew tired and out of breath, the Indian woman reappeared on the path in front of him, smiling. Did he really wish to follow this path?

After some time, several hours, they left the house and went to eat, shrimp and lemon grass soup with mushrooms, plain omelettes, stir-fried vegetables and sapota.

Lee opened up more, but the short of it was his posting was dull and boring. He had started smoking the opium occasionally to relieve the boredom, and the occasional smoke had grown into a habit.

Paul asked about the rumours of the hidden temples, Lee confirmed that these did exist, but were well-guarded secrets by the monks. He was able to tell Paul of some of the trails to start on, mumbling an excuse about being unable to go with him. Paul was relieved , tired after the O and the food. They parted company, and Paul went back to pack, sleep and get up early with the sun to follow the trails out of the village into the hills.

10

The Lizard's Veil

STEVE LOOKED AT THE MONK. He began to tell his story, in the same way that he had told Father Wallace.

'Ah, so your friend is not at rest.' It was said with the tone of a motor mechanic being told of a break-down.

'No, I guess not' said Steve.

'Your friend will be alright. He has been here, he knows of the temples, the other Buddhas, he knows that you will come here.' The monk was looking at Steve, smiling.

Steve felt shivers going up and down his spine.

'Your friend will rest now he knows you have made this journey for him. His death was an accident, and we will say prayers for him so that you both may rest.'

'What should I do?' asked Steve. The monk looked at him, smiled, but did not answer.

Paul followed the same paths up out of the village as

the monks and Steve. He guessed that the temples were hidden in the jungle up in the hills, protected by a sect of monks. He was curious.

He crossed a silver stream which flowed into the darkness of the Mekong. He followed the trail into the hills, where he was stopped short by three men dressed in the black cotton which Paul hadn't seen since he left Vietnam. They smiled as he approached, he smiled as they spoke to him in Thai. Paul shrugged his shoulders, and replied in Vietnamese. He guessed right, they spoke back in the same language. It was as if they had been expecting him, and they told him as much.

'How are your American paymasters?' asked the one on the left, the smaller of the three who reminded Paul of a cobra ready to strike. Lee, for some reason, had obviously set him up. He had to think fast, and find a way out. The odds were not good.

'I make use of the Americans, I work for myself.' He gambled. 'I was looking for some business in Chiangsaen. I couldn't find what I wanted so I've taken a few days break up here. The Americans have a lot of money for heroin,' he lied. 'My contact is away, maybe you could help?' Paul's heart was beating fast, his way out lay in knowing why Lee had set him up, but it made no sense. He guessed that the three Vietnamese were dealing arms and drugs and the possibility of American dollars might keep him alive.

'We could help you, or we could kill you. How much money have you got?'

'Ten thousand dollars, but there's more, much more. If you take this, we could meet back here if you could get the stuff. I need two or three kilos', he bluffed.

The cobra sat quietly. He looked at his companions. 'Give me the money!' he hissed.

Paul lifted his shirt slowly, removed a money belt from around his waist and handed it over. It was bulging, the Vietnamese were pleased.

'Three kilo?' asked the one next to Cobra.

'Yes. Three kilos, how much?'

'You pay American dollars, you bring another ten thousand dollars, we meet here in three days.'

Paul looked at them, and glanced down onto the money belt as they were fingering the notes. The sun glinted on an elephant ring on the right hand of the cobra, more precisely, it lit the large emerald which was seated between the two elephants, just as it had been the last time Paul had seen it, on his father's hand. There was no mistake, Paul knew that these silver rings weren't uncommon, but to find one with such an emerald in it was very rare. He remembered the story of how his father had the emerald set in the ring. 'The ring is a present from your mother, the stone belonged to your grandmother, I think they look well together don't you? I had the stone set in the ring the day after your mother agreed to marry me.' His father had worn it ever since. Paul remembered he could never get it off his finger, and knew that the Cobra would have had to cut it off.

'So, you can get the stuff?' asked Paul.

'We have the stuff. Can you get the money?'

Paul's mind was racing. 'I need more than three days, I need about a week. I have to go back down to Bangkok.' He thought for a minute one of them might decide to go with him, that he'd made a mistake. It turned out they weren't interested.

'So, we'll meet back here then in seven days about the same time?' asked Paul.

'Make sure you bring the money!' said the one next to the Cobra.

'Okay, no problem. I'd better go, I've got a lot to do. I'll see you in seven days, that's Sunday?'

Cobra nodded his head and Paul turned, setting out on the path back down the hill.

At an intersection of two paths he decided to turn back up the hill heading eastwards, away from the three Vietnamese. Never take the obvious route. He couldn't beat a path through the jungle anyway. His mind was still racing, did Lee know that these men were the murderers of his father, or was it pure coincidence? If Lee knew, he could have been well paid to set Paul up, but perhaps he was just short of money, and set him up anyway. You could never tell with junkies.

He walked for ten minutes or so crossing another stream. There was a noise on the path in front of him, footsteps approaching down the hill. His heart increased a beat, they must have guessed his change of direction and were following him, they didn't trust him. He dived underneath the shrouds of the dank vegetation, and waited, hot and nervous, with little time to think as the approaching footsteps grew louder.

Steve stayed with the monks for just a few more hours before setting off back down through the jungle. He felt that Mike was at rest. The calmness of the monk was mind-blowing, he needed a lot of time to reflect. He wanted to get back to Chiangsaen, and from there he didn't know. He thought he might stay a few days, go back up and visit the monks perhaps, or begin to head south.

Whilst the monastery was calm and peaceful, he found the jungle oppressive. He wasn't sure of his way, but headed downward. Like a hill climber coming down out of the mists and cloud, he thought he would eventually see his path clear before him. It was humid, he was sweating and began to feel tired for the first time since he had met the monks. He continued his path downhill for half an hour or so, when he came to a small intersection. Which way? He was heading down, this path crossed another path which seemed to circle round the hill. At some point it would either lead upwards, or descend further into the valley. Thinking that most paths up the hills are clockwise, he turned to his left. He continued for another fifteen or twenty minutes, but the width of the hill was such that the path remained more or less level.

The canopy of the jungle was so thick that no sun penetrated, the path was dark and not well trodden. At intervals the jungle had reclaimed parts of it, he thought he had reached a dead end.

The footsteps stopped. Paul then heard the noise of

someone cutting a swathe through. Cobra and co. were obviously confident, they made no attempt to be quiet. Their thrashing about grew louder and louder, Paul's heart pumped adrenaline round his body. His hands traced the outline of some one hundred dollar bills he had in small plastic bags sewn into the seams of his jacket, he followed the outline over his belt which concealed some gold sovereigns. He knew this was his best option, that the odds of one against three were bleak. He would try to buy some time with the extra dollars and gold, and then go for the cobra. His hand passed from his belt up underneath his right arm to the sheath which was home to a Fairburn Sykes commando knife. He had bought it when he was in England, a good weapon for the kill, nicely crafted with a good provenance.

Steve was having difficulty getting through the jungle in front of him. He was lying almost parallel to the ground, pulling himself through a small tunnel of undergrowth by grabbing hold of the branches in front of him and heaving himself forward towards what he thought was the path the other side. His kit kept getting snagged, but sweating and exhausted, he finally got through and almost fell onto the path.

In the semi-dark of the jungle floor, still peering from his hiding place, Paul saw a large shape drop to the ground in front of him. It got up, the outline of a westerner in dirty clothes as ragged as his own. It was a familiar shape, tall, athletic, broad shoulders. Paul's heart missed several beats, he leapt from the jungle and managed a 'Steve! Steve!'

Some twelve thousand miles from home, having spent the last several hours with a monk who seemed to chat with the dead on a regular basis, Steve was just a little surprised to see Paul leaping out from the jungle screaming his name. He was filthy dirty, and burned black by the sun.

'Paul? Paul?!'

'Steve! You're a long way from home!' Paul had recovered first. All the paranoia came back to Steve, and for a second in that dark jungle just south of Cambodia he was transported back into the darkness of the edge of the moor where worlds overlapped.

'Paul! Mike's dead!' he blurted.

'Jesus! What happened?'

'Too much acid I guess. It was after you left, you know, we'd been on the beach and you went off with Ian. Then, uh, Mike went up to a festival and took a load of purple microdot that he found. Maybe it was bad acid, I dunno, anyway he had a bad trip and he never came down.'

'Shit! He was never really a guy who should have taken that stuff. How did he die?'

A good question. As far as the police were concerned, the verdict was death by misadventure, and Steve had always felt that for once they had got it right. Definitely misadventure. 'He jumped out of a train.'

'Shit! Did he mean to?'

'Well, I don't think he thought he was on his way to the restaurant car.'

The monks had given Steve some strength, he turned the tables. 'So what are you doing here Paul?'

Steve had the edge, it nudged Paul towards responsibility for his friend's death, however unfounded.

'Well, you know, just travelling. It is, after all, my neck of the woods.'

'Neck of the woods', an interesting turn of phrase, thought Steve. Paul, as ever, was the biggest question mark in his life. What was he really doing here?

'Look' said Paul, 'I'm heading down towards Chiangsaen. Why don't we travel down together, maybe we could spend a few days there and hang around, catch up on what's been happening?'

Steve had no option.

Paul decided to play it straight, that is as straight as he could, which meant telling Steve what he thought he needed to know to get him to do what he wanted. He still needed lieutenants, perhaps one to help set up an operation in Thailand. He could double by keeping an eye on the local traffic, and Lee. He would have to deal with him at some point.

'Well I'd better tell you what I've been doing, and fill in some gaps. I should start with my parents,' opened Paul. 'My father was killed when I was very young, when I was still a child really. He was a Frenchman, as you know, but my mother was actually Vietnamese, not Indian. I'm sorry about that. My father was tortured to death by the V.C.' Paul paused to let the full impact of this sink in.

'Jesus Christ!'

'After that, my mother went to live in Paris and later on I went to college in the States. After I finished college, I just wanted to start travelling and came over to Europe. Then I was gonna go into Turkey and through Afghanistan into India, you know. When I left you guys it was because I'd heard a rumour that it wasn't actually the V.C. who tortured and killed my father but some smack dealers who had been trying to get him to ship some stuff back to France with the rubber we exported, that was my father's business.' Paul paused again to see how the story was doing.

'So you were brought up in Vietnam then?'

'Yeah. Yeah until I went to the States and I spent a bit of time in France and Europe, travelling around. The guys who killed my father were supposed to have come from Laos back into Thailand to wash the money they got from the smack deals.'

'So did you find them?'

'No, it was a false trail, you know how these things start. It was from an old Vietnamese servant of my mother's who travelled to France to see her, and he told her about all the deals that had been going on, and the new heroin trade. He said that my father had known about it and had tried to stop it, and that was why he had been executed. The blame was then put on the V.C., then the war had been growing anyway and he was forgotten about. Then this old servant saw one of the guys back in Saigon and that was how he came to tell my mother. Through friends and relatives we found out that the guy sometimes came to Bangkok and had an address there and that's how I ended up in Thailand.'

'Jesus! So your father was really murdered by smack dealers.'

'Yeah.' Paul thought for a second about Sam, about the Agency. He wondered if they had actually contracted the murder to set him up as a recruit.

'Yeah. His death sort of cast me adrift, and it's difficult for me to go back to the war. But what about you Steve, how did you get here?'

Like Paul, Steve too had been thinking on his way down the hill. He decided that he would simply tell Paul he wanted to do some travelling and that he had decided to start in the Far East, head back through India and Turkey to the UK, then home. He said he thought he might go round the other way, out to Sydney and over to California, he wasn't sure. He was looking for waves, but he had met a girl in the UK. They arrived back at the village, walking the last part in silence.

'You wanna get stoned?' asked Paul after Steve had told him his tale. 'I've got some Thai sticks, it's nice grass.'

'Sure. Why not? I've got a room not too far from here, we could go up there, it's cool.'

Paul rolled a small joint, took a few hits, and passed it to Steve. 'Just like old times!' he said smiling. And so it was. In the Chiaroscuro of the small room as the sun went down, flickering shadows played upon Paul's face as if a magic swayed gently around him. Paul spoke.

'You know when I was at college in the States, I was

144

approached by a guy who turned out worked for the D.E.A., and he told me if ever I came back over here they might have a small job for me. I guess the guy had done his homework pretty well, he knew how my Pa had been killed and that I already had a motive. Anyway, I took him up on his offer. I thought it might help me track down my father's killers and also, well, you know,' Paul smiled and fixed his eyes on Steve, 'There's money. Just for hanging around and telling them a little bit about any smack deals or anything I hear of, they help finance my travels. I got some other business going as well which is about stories from home, I mean 'Nam. I tell the T.V. crews and journalists what's going on, you know, because I speak the language, and they keep me in funds as well.'

Steve was stoned, he wasn't quite sure what Paul was saying. Paul continued. 'There's a big future out here man. When the war's over you'll see. The East is gonna open up, it's gonna be huge. There are fantastic chances here for us to have a really cool life and make an awful lot of money!' He wondered if money was still a dirty word to the American.

'So how would that involve me?' asked Steve.

'Well I have to go back and forwards, you know, to Saigon. It would be really useful to have somebody set up over here who I could trust and keep an eye on things for me.' He continued. 'I have a house in Bangkok. It needs looking after and I have some business connections there, Thais, who invest some of the dollars for me and I wanna get something together with them.

I'm not quite sure yet, may be stones, may even start a hotel or something. I think Thailand could be a big tourist place in the future. Interested?'

Steve thought of Kate, Father Wallace, of the long dark nights when Paul had never been far from his mind. Now, here in front of him, weaving his magic, he wondered had he been mistaken? Paul, after all, was bound to be weird just from things that had happened to him. Paul's offer, on face value, was attractive. But what about Kate? Maybe she could come out and join him, they could spend long hot nights together in Bangkok, travelling up to the north and the quiet of the hills when the city became too much.

Paul was rolling another joint.

'It's a bit hard to take in' said Steve.

Paul's mind was racing. He kept thinking of the ring, had the cobra been the one? Maybe he had just come by it, maybe they weren't the ones. But he felt that all the pieces fitted together too well for him to escape this simple twist of fate. Or not so simple. Had the Agency set him up? Did they know what he'd been up to? He needed to keep Steve around, but he had to concentrate on the next meeting up in the hills in seven days time. If Lee had set him up, then he could do it again. He could dump Steve on Lee for a while, tell Lee what had happened as if he didn't suspect, go back up to the hills and then? Paul would still have to have some proof that these were the ones who had tortured and killed his father. The only way he would get any proof was to get a confession, to somehow trick them into it.

'Tell you what' said Paul 'I've gotta go back down to Bangkok in a few days, why don't you come with me and you can meet my Thai friends there. See how you get on with them, and decide then.' He smiled at Steve and passed him the joint.

Steve was relieved, took the joint, took a toke and held the smoke deep in. As he exhaled he said 'okay.'

Two days later they stood together outside the Thai Farmers Bank in Bangkok.

Paul liked to stay up-market. 'Always go up-market if you can, it's more anonymous', he said. This time Paul had taken it to an extreme, they were staying at the Oriental. Even in the States Steve had never seen such luxury. Paul seemed very relaxed amongst it, having bought himself and Steve full sets of new clothing on leaving the bank. He had also bought Samsonite suit-cases, four of them, each identical.

'I'll show you how to do cases' he said enigmatically. He then dragged Steve around some ironmongery shops to buy glue, craft tool knives, scissors, electrical tape, plastic bags and some latex gloves from a pharmacy. They had separate rooms. 'Otherwise they'll think I'm on the game!' joked Paul, and they gathered the kit together in Steve's room.

'In this business we need to be able to move things around like currency and stones. Otherwise, you know, if customs find you with a lot of cash they'll just take it off you. This is one of the easiest ways to do it, making cases.'

He opened one of the empty Samsonites and carefully levered up the metal rim which housed the bottom part of the case. He did it with a screwdriver covered by the electrical tape. He then stood on the bottom of the case and snapped it away from the metal. He did the same thing to a second case and then cut off about three centimetres from the top edge all the way round. From a money belt strapped round his waist he produced a huge amount of dollars which he put into the plastic bags before he laid them flat in the bottom of the original case. He then placed the second case bottom on top of this and in a period of about fifteen minutes glued this and the original case bottom into the metal rim of the first case.

Paul looked up 'To do the job properly you really need to seal the dollars in and glue the edges. I just did this one quickly to show you roughly how it's done.' He had recreated a perfect empty Samsonite suitcase containing in its false bottom approximately thirty thousand dollars. It could have contained obviously quite a few other things, and Steve wondered if the killers of Paul's father were the only smack dealers Paul knew of. Paul read his thoughts. 'Sure. It's an old smugglers trick. Trouble is, out here you can't trust anybody so it's as well to be safe, it's a lot of money!'

'What's it for?' asked Steve.

'Like I said, I want to trade with it. Stones are cheap here, sometimes we have to use the cases to move currency into places like Burma. Well, you know, even in Europe they have currency restrictions. Why don't you have a go?'

Steve did, it took him about an hour to get to the first stage of trimming the three centimetres off the bottom of the first case. Paul laughed. 'I've had a bit more practice than you!' He finished the cases off, leaving the bottom of the second one empty.

'What about the gloves?' asked Steve.

'Ah, they're for another time.'

Steve was tempted. Paul had more money than he'd dreamed of, and he would have had to have been dead from the neck up not to have got off on what Paul was up to, or said he was up to. Again, there was the question mark hanging over Paul.

It was evening, they dined in the hotel and Paul left to set up a meeting for the following day with his contacts in Bangkok. Steve sat alone in his room, thinking about Kate, the monks, Mike, everything that had happened since arriving in the East. From his room in the Oriental its tapestry stretched out in front of him, through Paul he had a way through the impenetrable. He would never have the chance again, never the chance to make the sort of money on offer, the chance to actually live disconnected from his own past, free.

Paul was late. They'd agreed to meet in his room at around eleven. Steve waited until 11.30 p.m. and then left a note for Paul saying that he was going to sleep. He dreamed of dark mountains leading down to the sea, emerald fields and white seagulls. A small stone-built shepherds' church nestled in the hills, he walked in between a narrow row of dark pews, the oak polished black over centuries of use. At the far end was a rood screen with elaborate faces and patterns carved upon the wood. As he walked towards it, Paul emerged carrying a candle and walking towards the altar. In the distance he heard what sounded like the bleating of a lamb or the crying of a baby. As he approached, Paul stepped further towards the alter on which an emerald Buddha sat. They were alone, but as Steve turned, he saw a glimpse of a monk through the small opening in the walls. He left to follow the monk, who turned and faced him. It was Mike. 'Hi, how long have you been here?' he asked.

'I've just arrived' said Steve.

'It's cool here. You'll like it, c'mon I'll show you round' he said and they walked off together down one of the paths into the forest.

Breakfast at the Oriental was an exotic affair. Paul had got back in the early hours of the morning, and they both ate Thai style. 'I've gotta leave for Saigon in about three days' said Paul blandly. 'I'm not sure how long I'll be gone. I've talked to my contacts here, they have agreed for me to give you their address, if you want to you can go and see them. They'll have a bit of work for you. I think it will probably be taking some stones to a Dutch guy here. He'll give you dollars and you just have to go back with the cash. Straightforward.'

Not uncharacteristically Paul had manoeuvred Steve into a position. The tension of the delay, the setting in the Oriental was stage-managed, like the night on the edge of the moors.

'Here's their address,' he said pulling it out from his

top pocket, 'and here's the address of my house in Bangkok. There's a girl there who comes and cleans, she's cool, she'll take care of you and if you need anything, she'll take care of you. Oh, and you'll need some funds.'

Paul had been thorough. He wanted Steve on board, but he knew it wouldn't work if he didn't seem to make the choice for himself.

'I've got some work to do before I go, I'll be with my Thai friends if you need me. We need to check out by mid-day, I was gonna go straight over to them, and I guess you could go on over to my house if you like.'

Steve took the money and the addresses. He had nothing to lose by doing so. Paul had left him a way out, he could choose to be there when Paul came back, working with his contact, or be somewhere else. He had no idea which it would be.

Paul had five days left to get back up to Chiangsaen and prepare himself for the meet in the hills. How to make sure that these were his father's killers was the burning question. The second question was, if they were, what would he do about it? If he could get proof, did he have the right to take their lives in return? Would not Karma take care of them, further on down the road? He thought that would be the best solution, but then again, no. Also there was the possibility that the Agency was getting rid of him. Maybe it had paid them to off his father, and now it was his turn, he'd outgrown his usefulness. He thought for a long time. He decided to try and trick them into telling him the story of the ring, how they got it.

He decided to go through the motions of revenge in the event that he had proof they were the ones. If he was going to carry out what would in effect be an execution, it needed a lot of preparation. Initially he thought an automatic weapon concealed in a holdall bag could do the trick, but then, they might find it. He thought of poison, maybe they could celebrate the deal with a drink. Not very characteristic. He could use an accomplice, it was going to be difficult enough to kill three of them as it was. But who? Despite the whats and ifs, the more he thought about actually doing it, the more he got into it, the more it seemed the right thing to do, and the only proviso was the proof.

In the end he decided to go up to the hills straight away, to the R.V. He planned to dig pits six feet deep in a semi-circle around the meeting place, and ram home punji stakes like the V.C. used, so sharp that they went through the boots of the grunts when they fell into them. In this case they would be sharp enough to go through the body of anyone who fell onto them. Paul figured that if he managed to get them into the pits and they weren't killed by the sticks, he could finish them off with a sidearm.

Twenty-four hours later he was in Chiangsaen. He rested the night, and got up early heading up into the hills for the R.V. He was two days early, and allowed himself this amount of time to do the digging and preparatory work. He knew the digging would be gruesomely hard. He had brought two picks, a shovel, gloves, a large machete, string, a large bush knife and an MC-1 parachutist knife as well as the old Fairbyrne Sykes which he kept in a sheath in the small of his back. He took some rations up with him, and hoped to be able to top up with water from the streams which fed the Mekhong.

The digging was hard, as hard as he had expected. The difficult part though was yet to come, the insertion of the stakes so that they were solid enough to take the full weight of a falling body, and concealment of the pits afterwards.

Fortunately the ambient light beneath the canopy of the jungle was not particularly bright, no shafts of sunlight would be searching out the imperfections in his work. When the pit was dug he drove in the stakes by sharpening one end and using the sledge hammer on the other end to drive it in. He then used his machete to trim off the other ends roughly, sharpened them up a bit more with the bush knife and finished the tips with the MC-1. He liked MC-1's, and like all his kit this one had been kept in first class nick. He finished off the tips and thought about the V.C. doing this in the jungle back home, around the highlands of Dak, or along the paths through the elephant grass south east of Saigon. He thought of his other school friends, some from the States, who would be stepping down onto them. He covered the pits with a criss cross of young fresh cut bamboo and some cheap cotton netting he bought in Chiangsaen. He didn't kid himself that his skills were up to those of the V.C., and he needed every helping hand he could get. The netting worked a treat, and he meticulously replaced the surface of the jungle floor he had swept away.

All he had to do now was wait. If the smack dealers were going to be on time, that meant about twelve hours. He checked his kit. He checked it again. He looked at the pits again, he thought through the positioning of it all, how he would get them onto the pits. He had left a narrow path in the middle of two of them and his plan was that he would walk or run along this with them following, but the path was so narrow they would go to one side of it or the other. It was simple, but it should work so long as they were chasing him. Anything else would have been too complicated because this enemy was too unpredictable. Would they turn up? How would he know for sure it was they who killed his father?

He ate some biscuits, some fruit and finished off the last of the water he had brought up with him. He refilled from one of the streams, and concealed himself and his kit about thirty metres from the pits, near a tree trunk. He stretched out, covered his face with a bit of mosquito netting and tried to sleep. Actually, he lay listening to every noise. In the end he sat up cross-legged and used a mantra to meditate. In this way he could relax his body a little, and his mind, but still be able to take in what was going on around him. What if? As dawn began to penetrate the canopy of the jungle, doubt crossed his mind. His problem was the enemy, their unpredictability, but the 'what ifs' were too late, he'd been through most of them and come up with this. The die was cast. He was hungry, he finished off the biscuits and waited. Had his father waited back at home, north of Saigon, for the same men?

He needed to take a leak. He got up, away from the tree trunk and his kit. He walked towards the stream and unbuttoned his fly. He was in mid stream when he heard them. The pits were in a semi-circle on the north-east side, he had rested on the south side, and they were approaching from the west. He needed to get back towards the north, to their original meeting place near his kit, so he stopped, wetting his trousers as he got his tackle back inside his pants. He moved quickly back to pick up his bag then turned round to walk up towards the pits. They arrived at the spot at almost exactly the same time, which put them on edge.

'I was early' said Paul. 'Just been for a leak down by the stream.'

Cobra looked at the splash marks down the front of Paul's trousers. 'You got the money?' said Cobra, courteous to a fault.

'Sure. You got the stuff?' said Paul.

He laughed. 'You wanna try it?'

'No, not my thing. But I brought some American bourbon from Bangkok, do you want to try some?' Paul moved to get into his bag, the smack dealers started but let him carry on. He brought out a bottle and handed it over. They all took a long glug each. Paul thought of the poison, it would have been easy.

'Let's sit down shall we?' he said. He manoeuvred

himself about five metres to the south of the left hand pit and they sat down opposite him. If the path had continued down they would have been sitting on either side of it. So far so good.

'How much did you bring?' asked Paul. 'Three kilos?'

'Yes, three kilo here.' said the one Paul mentally called number three.

'Can I see?'

'The money?'

Paul reached for his bag but number three reached out and snatched it from him, smiling. He turned it upside down on the dirt, and the contents spilled out between them. A drinking bottle, T-shirt, toothbrush, a small length of rope, the paper from the biscuits, a towel and a map. No money. 'It's in the side pocket' said Paul, and it was. He had buried the rest of the kit, the shovels, pick axes, in the pits. The dealers were pleased. 'How much?'

'Another ten thousand dollars, some of it on account for the next time' said Paul. Cobra took the money and as he fingered it Paul looked again at the ring. There was no mistake.

'That's a very beautiful ring. How much would you sell it for?'

'It's not for sale. I went to a lot of trouble to get it!' the Cobra laughed.

'And how was that?' asked Paul, smiling.

'I cut it off the finger of some French bastard who asked too many questions like you!'

Paul laughed. 'No more questions! But I will still

156

need to get some more stuff in three weeks or so, next time I'll need more, maybe four, five kilos.'

'That's another fifteen thousand dollars.'

Paul was angry, his heart was thumping like a sledge-hammer. He felt round his back, his hand slipping onto the familiar handle of the Fairburn Sykes. He whipped it out from its sheath.

'What did you cut the finger off with, my friend, something like this?'

The dealers were non-plussed. They were too arro-gant to move, they simply looked at each other. What would they do? Slice him up slowly, or just shoot him? It seemed as though they thought Paul was half screw-ing around, they couldn't quite take him for real. It was what he needed, and he sliced the cobra vertically down from his eye, outwards across his cheekbone and then horizontally back across the throat. The knife was so sharp it cut the flesh through to the bones on the cheek, before it tore across the neck, slicing the inter-nal jugular vein. The result was quite dramatic, and blood sprayed like water from a garden hose, splatter-ing the other two bandits. They were pissed off. Paul legged it, straight across the narrow path between the pits and they were in hot pursuit swearing at him and fumbling for their guns and knives as they chased him.

As soon as Paul got to the northern edge of the first pit he turned sharp left so that they could head him off by cutting across the pit. They did, and gravity took over. Number Two seemed to somehow carry on run-ning into the pit so that one of the stakes went up between his legs and came out through his stomach. Cobra must have tripped as he went into the pit and somehow seemed to go spread-eagled as if he was free-falling. In a sense he was. One stake got him between the eyes, another one through the thigh. He was killed instantly. Number Two took a bit longer to die, giving Paul time to tell him that the Frenchman with the ring had been his father.

Paul threw the heroin into the pit with the three of them, and the rest of their gear. He took the money they had on them and retrieved the ten thousand dollars he had just handed over. In all he must have collected somewhere between thirty and forty thousand dollars. He knew plenty of orphans back in Saigon who could get an education with that sort of money. He cut the tips from the rest of the stakes in both pits, and pulled out the ones which were loose enough. The worst that would happen to anyone who fell in there would be a nasty shock, whether or not they took some smack to get over it would be up to them. Finally, he took his father's ring from the cobra's corpse. He would need to go to Paris with it, and return it to his mother. Hopefully, if Steve started to pick up some of the threads in Thailand, it would free him up.

Secret World

STEVE WAS GLAD TO HAVE some time alone when Paul had left. He thought over Paul's story, and most of it made sense. Now that he was in the East he could see how Paul fitted in. He thought more about Mike and felt that he was at rest. What had Father Wallace been up to? What about Kate?

In one sense the purpose of his journey had been achieved. He felt his friend had found peace, and the unanswered questions about his death and Paul were now only relevant in so far as Paul had re-surfaced. Steve could live for a thousand years and never unravel the secrets held by the monks. There were many levels, he felt as if he was simply at the gate of a secret garden. Paul had undoubtedly journeyed through parts of it. Were there dark forces out there? Father Wallace certainly seemed to think so. Was Paul part of them? Bearing in mind what Steve now knew, he felt that in some ways Paul acted as a type of transmitter; he suspected that the transmissions were not always conscious, and Paul had further to go before he himself would fully grasp the gifts that he had.

Thinking that there are more questions in life than answers, he made his way over to Paul's house in Bangkok. He took a river taxi near the Oriental, bargained hard and felt he wasn't getting ripped off too badly. From the river he made his way by taxi heading north and then east to an indistinguished residential area in the old part of town. The house looked equally indistinguished, walking towards the entrance, he felt he had been expected. A small beautiful Thai girl greeted him in English, 'Hello, you must be Paul's friend?' She seemed to embody the charm of Thailand, and any doubts or fears of staying at Paul's simply vanished. 'Please, come in.' Steve took off his shoes, left his bag just inside the entrance and was escorted into a deceptively large room. 'My name is Thoy' she said.

'Thoy?'

'Yes. Thoy.'

Paul had not scrimped with his wealth. Teak wall panelling and beams provided a backdrop to some impressive furniture and artefacts.

'I will show you your room' said Thoy. She gave him a tour of the house which had several rooms, two of which were as large as the reception room. Paul's room and study were locked but the rest of the house was open and as beautifully furnished as the first. One room was dedicated to a library, the bedrooms had French wardrobes, large vases, Chinese rugs, Thai silk, and a great deal of Burmese lacquer-wear which he must have brought down from the border. Most of the rooms had a Buddha facing inwards from the window, and there were two impressionist oil paintings in one of the larger rooms, one signed by Pisarro. There was also some very up to the minute hi-fi and a phenomenal number of albums. Steve wondered what Paul had locked away in his room. He guessed the house had been chosen so that from the exterior its size was not obvious.

'Would you like some food?' asked Thoy. 'I was going to cook some vegetables, and some rice.'

'Yeah, that would be great' said Steve.

'Ah, excuse me, I forgot to show you the guests' bathroom.'

This proved to be an elaborate affair, a large sunken bath, pedestal washbasin, w.c., bidet and a mosaic floor patterned with elephants and palms. There were fresh houseplants in terracotta pots, and a large window which looked out onto the canal. The mosquito netting had been fitted in the French style of mousti-quaires, and the panels had been removed so that from the bath it was possible to gaze out over the dark green waters. 'Not too many mosquitoes this time of year' said Thoy, reading his thoughts.

'Well, guess I'll take a bath and then we can eat' said Steve.

He lolled around in the bath, and turned on the hot tap with his left toe. He gazed out of the window over the canal and thought of Kate. Then he thought of Thoy, and wondered what would happen as the meal drew to a close. He would leave it up to her, but guessed that Paul meant what he said when he told him that she would provide whatever he needed. Looking at the Buddha, he was, he decided, as yet unliberated by the four noble truths. He consoled himself with the thought that he was still young and had plenty of time to practice, and his mind began to wander over the curves of Thoy's body.

There was a knock at the door. His heart rate increased. 'Come in' he heard himself say. She came in and he shifted one or two inches further into the water. She smiled.

'Would you like me to wash you?'

Does Jerry Garcia play the guitar?

'I was uh ... um ...' She laughed. 'Ah, Paul said you like to smoke. Would you prefer it if I went to roll a joint for you?'

'Yeah, yeah that would be great, I was-uh-just getting out you know.' She had in any case saved face for him.

'Do you want to smoke opium or just some hash?'

'Ah, some hash would be fine. Where did you learn to speak English so perfectly?' he asked.

'From Paul.' she smiled. 'So, I'll see you in a minute, in the large room near your bedroom, the one with the French paintings in it.' She left the room and he got out, dried himself and put on a black towelling robe which she had left there for him. How far did Paul's friendship go? Was she his woman? Was she there to make sure he joined up with him? He thought of Kate again. His conscience was a real nuisance, still, what the eye can't see, anyway, how did he know Kate was being faithful to him?

The meal was all it promised to be. He was stoned anyway so he had the appetite of a wolf. The dope was also working on his hormones and Thoy looked even more beautiful.

'I have made some takoh! It is a kind of coconut cream' she said. Steve was trying not to seem like a greedy barbarian.

'Um, sounds intriguing' he smiled.

They liked each other. He was a big, and to her, probably ugly farang, but now that he'd had a bath perhaps he didn't smell too badly. She liked the way he tried not to be embarrassed, the way he tried not to embarrass her, he was like a big ape with a kind heart.

'Have you been in Thailand a very long time?' She asked with the emphasis on the very, granting him face.

'No, just a short while actually, I like it very much.'

'I will fetch the takoh!'

She was right, it was a kind of coconut cream and Steve liked it very much. He tried desperately not to shovel it in, but still managed to finish ahead of her. As always when he ate Thai food, he felt full but not overly so. The relatively small portions somehow always satisfied him.

'Would you like some tea?' asked Thoy, after she had finished her dessert.

'Yes, thank you' he answered, trying not to look at the outline of her breasts in the fine silk kimono she was wearing. She noticed anyway. 'Ah, you are looking at my kimono! Paul gave it to me, it is a very old one which he bought from a Japanese in Bangkok. Would you prefer to drink some coffee and cognac instead of tea? I know Paul likes cognac very much, a taste he inherited from his father I think. He has some very old ones here, would you like to try?'

Yes, thought Steve, I would like to try. 'Yes, thank you, that would be lovely' he smiled. As Thoy got up the kimono seemed to cling to the shape of her body, the silk was so delicate it covered her like fine mist over the hills, as if with the slightest breath it would melt away. Paul's words echoed around his mind. 'She'll take care of you and if you need anything, and I mean anything, she'll arrange it.' How carefully had he chosen his words? Arrange? Thoy came back in, carrying a Burmese lacquered tray with a bottle of Courvoisier X.O. and one brandy glass. He was careful to point his feet away from her as she entered the room, respecting the Thai custom whilst he remained seated. She, on the other hand, came extremely close to him as she placed the tray beside him, and for a second her kimono brushed his cheek. Knowing a little of the Thais' respect for space, he thought this must have been deliberate. Her perfume reminded him of magnolias in the spring time, heady, narcotic. She avoided touching him after she put the tray down, leaving the perfume in her place.

'I'll fetch the tea and coffee' she said. 'Oh, and Paul left some sticks of grass for you, he said you liked them, shall I bring them in too?'

She stood in the doorway, he sat motionless for a second before he could reply. 'Yes, thanks.' He picked up the pear-shaped bottle of Courvoisier, and poured a large measure into the glass. He held it for several seconds, and sipped it, held the glass in both hands and sipped again, letting its warm glow spread through his body. He sat alone in this way for several minutes, waiting for her return. His heart was beating faster, the cognac and grass mixing now with his own adrenaline which began to flow in anticipation. Where was she? Her perfume lingered in the air, he poured himself another glass.

From Chiangsaen Paul scurried like a beetle across the red earth back to the dark comfort of Bangkok. He checked in at the Oriental, picked up one of the cases he had left there before going up north, and after a long shower changed into some of the fresh clothes which had been immaculately laundered by the hotel. He drank an ice cold beer, and got rid of the clothes he had been wearing by dumping them in a perforated plastic bag which he weighed down with stones and threw into the river close to the hotel. He went back to his room, put all the dollars into the false bottom of the case, packed some more carefully around his body, drank another beer and took a taxi up to near his house.

He thought about Steve, he liked him, knowing that he possessed the rarest quality in the world, he could be trusted.

He got out of the taxi at the same spot as Steve,

although the fare he paid was half. As his feet touched the shore he sensed that Steve had been there before, but what he called his father's mind, the rational mind, told him it was probably wishful thinking. The lights were on as he approached his house, Thoy switched them on in his absence as a precaution, although she was well able to defend herself. He had met her three years earlier in Bangkok, fighting in the street with a meat cleaver, taking revenge on some Chinese she claimed had killed her brother in a business quarrel. He sympathized. They became lovers, but Paul at this time in his life was unable to remain entirely faithful. 'Why do you think they put one cockerel in with several hens?' said an old Thai friend of his. It never answered the question for Paul but somehow the phrase stuck in his mind. Later he and Thoy became like sister and brother, neither of them really taking other lovers, so that a question mark hung over this area of their lives.

As always he approached the house with caution. He never used the front door, he walked in through the gate and left his bag in the bushes on the left-hand side to free his hands should he need them. He then moved cautiously towards the house, avoiding the beams of light which stabbed at the shadows. It was silent.

Thoy thought she would in any case prepare a pipe of opium for her guest. She would take it in with the coffee. Paul had several pipes, silver and beautifully carved, but he seldom smoked. 'It's not really my thing,' he would say. Thoy never smoked, she didn't approve but she knew that many of the Farangs in

Thailand liked it, and she didn't mind because it made the foul-smelling giants more docile. She thought about Paul, and whilst accustomed to his frequent disappearances was surprised at the most recent one. She had expected him to be here, with her, with no farang. She knew this man was important to Paul, and she would do everything to help him, but why?

She was puzzling over this as she finished preparing the pipe and began to pour the coffee from a blue Dutch cafetière, a present from one of Paul's friends in Amsterdam.

'You should be more careful!' said a familiar voice behind her.' Her heart leapt as she turned round to see Paul standing only three or four feet behind her, looking clean and fresh.

'Why do you always do that?! We're not children anymore, you want me to grow old quickly?!'

Paul laughed. 'Like I said, you should be more careful! You left the back door open again.'

'Been cooking, it was to just freshen the air a little, I was about to close it.' She looked a little sheepish. Paul looked at the coffee and the pipe.

'You told me you didn't like that stuff' he teased.

'You know who it's for! He's very nice, your farang friend. Is he staying?'

'I don't know. I want him to. I want him to be my general here. What do you think?'

Thoy knew Paul would do what he wanted, whatever she thought.

'I haven't got to know him yet' she teased back.

Paul smiled. 'Give me the tray then, I'll surprise him!'

Steve was on his third cognac. He thought he'd go and find out where Thoy was, but then his imagination was running riot. Maybe she was changing into something even more comfortable, but how more comfortable could she get? He kept thinking about Kate and the more he tried not to the more her laugh, her quick temper, flashed across his mind. Shit. Love the one you're with. The dope was making him paranoid too, maybe Paul was really setting him up and this was a honey trap. He got a grip, gulped the brandy, and let his mind wander again over the curves of Thoy's body. He heard footsteps through the hallway coming from the kitchen. At last! His imagination still getting the better of him, he thought he'd better avert his eyes, wait until she approached him. She got closer, he could hear the chinking of the coffee cups, its heavy aroma covering the lingering trails of her perfume. His heart was thumping hard now.

'Hi man! How you doing?' said Paul in a semi-accusatory tone.

'Jesus!' Steve jumped up spilling the brandy as he spun round to face Paul, standing there cool as the evening surf. 'What are you doing here?' was all he could feebly ask.

'Well, it is my house and I was feeling a little tired, hope you don't mind.' He read Steve's thoughts. 'Thoy is still in the kitchen making some more coffee, it seems she'd only made enough for two.' Steve was melting.

'It's a really beautiful house, Paul. I think I'd be tempted to live here all the time if it was mine!'

Paul let him off the hook. 'Why don't you? Why don't you live here all the time?' He was smiling, grinning, as the penny began to slowly tumble through Steve's mind.

He laughed. 'Jesus!'

Thoy came in from the kitchen, bringing some more coffee and the pipe she had prepared earlier. She smiled warmly at Steve.

'Paul said perhaps you might stay with us for some time?'

'Well let's talk about that later' said Paul. 'I'll get some more glasses.'

He left the room and came back with two more brandy glasses, some champagne glasses and a bottle of Krug in an ice bucket. 'Thoy doesn't really like coffee or brandy, but she does manage to drink this once in a while, don't you?' he said, turning his attention to her.

'Um, I sure do!' she laughed 'it's one of the French habits I like very much. We can drink it any time can't we!'

Steve hadn't quite fully recovered, but he felt much more relaxed now. The mantle had been set aside between him and Paul, he had never felt such warmth from Paul before. Still, his caution, paranoia, was alive and twitching. Was this to be a ménage à trois? Paul spoke, 'Well I suggest we have a few glasses of this' he said pointing to the Krug. 'A few pipes of this' he said pointing to the opium pipe, 'and then personally I'm going to sleep, to sleep the sleep of the devil!' Steve's heart jumped again, but he was too far down the line

171

now. He reached for an opium pipe, and offered it to Thoy. She declined, preferring to stay with the champagne. He offered it to Paul.

'Sure, why not?! It's not my thing really, but I wouldn't mind some tonight, I've had a busy day!'

Steve lit the pipe for him. Paul smoked it all himself, and repeated the operation for Steve. It made him feel nauseous, on top of the brandy, the hash and the champagne he had glugged whilst trying to calm down. He went pale and Paul noticed. 'Not bad O eh?' Steve managed to nod his head before lying flat out, stretched across the floor at an angle, his head forgetting itself and pointing towards Thoy. Paul had done the same thing the other side of her, and she sat between the two of them sipping the champagne.

Steve dreamed of a dark forest, where streams of blood fed a wide black lake. There were three swans upon it, and they cried out. As they opened their beaks, silver moths spread their wings from inside and scattered like snow beneath the full moon. The moon turned crimson, the moths disappeared, melting away, and he walked among black tulips on the shores of the lake.

The early morning sun filtered through the moustiquaires which Thoy had replaced at some point during the night. Steve was alone in the big room where he had crashed out the night before. He felt as if his mind had been washed clean, he felt warm and relaxed. He was lying staring at the ceiling, enjoying this feeling when Thoy came in bringing with her the blue cafetière and some croissants.

'It's a French breakfast this morning!' she said, smiling. Steve was hungry again, he sat up and she poured a cafe au lait into a large cup.

'Thanks!' smiled Steve.

'How did you sleep?' she asked, cunningly.

He laughed. 'Pretty well I guess!'

'Well, I'll let you get on with your breakfast, I've put another robe out for you in the guests' bathroom and there's a clean set of clothes too. Paul's gone out but he'll be back soon.' She would have liked to have sat with him while he came to, but she'd seen Farangs dip the croissants into the coffee, and watched on occasions as they fished out lumps of them with their fingers.

'Thanks' he smiled at her, and she smiled back.

The coffee was excellent and the croissants were fresh and still warm. He didn't like to dunk them in coffee, so Thoy would, in any case, have been spared. He showered, changed into the beautifully laundered clothes and found her sitting in the large reception room sipping green tea. He heard the front door close, and some shuffling in the hallway. Paul joined them, looking irritatingly fresh.

'Hi!' he uttered. 'Hmm! Any more tea?'

'I'll make some more.' Thoy tactfully disappeared towards the kitchen and Paul got straight down to business.

'So, have you thought anymore about my offer. I mean it, I can trust you. I don't really trust anyone else, except Thoy. I need someone here, it's getting too complicated for me to handle everything, and I have to go off all the time over to 'Nam or up north here. It would be good, your being an American, a lot of my contacts are guys in the forces or whatever, and when the war's over, like I said, Thailand's going to really open up. A Thai speaking American could do well for himself here!'

Paul looked cunningly at Steve. Steve felt the offer was genuine, his paranoia, if that's what it had been, was less acute in the warmth of the morning. 'Well that's an offer that's hard to refuse! Look, you know there are some things going on for me in the U.K., I'd really need to sort all that out.'

'You mean the girl?' asked Paul.

'Yeah.' Steve also thought of Father Wallace and Mike, the purpose for his journey. He needed to close the circle.

'Okay, well there's no rush. I've got to go to Paris. Why don't you stay here for a while, I'll be away for about ten days and when I'm back we can talk some more?'

'Okay, sounds good!'

At that moment Thoy came back into the room with yet another lacquered tray, this time bearing tea and fruit. Paul seemed anxious to get on. Usually when speaking with him, Steve realized in hindsight that Paul had already thought through everything they were talking about, but this time it seemed as if he was shooting from the hip.

'I'm going to Paris for a while Thoy, to see my mother

174

and sort out some business there.' He may as well have said he was popping round the corner to get a loaf of bread, she was obviously so used to his comings and goings. Whilst she didn't take him for granted, she accepted them with the equanimity which came from an understanding both of the relationship and the ebb and flow of life.

'I have some silks which your mother would like, you mustn't go without them!' She smiled at Paul. 'When is your flight?'

'It's this evening actually.'

Thoy knew there were no scheduled flights at that time out of Bangkok to Europe. She guessed he would have been using what she called his private plane, he would be lying in the back of one of the huge camouflaged Hercules which occasionally droned over the northern skies of Thailand. They always made her afraid. She turned to Steve.

'Are you staying for a while then?'

'Well, I guess we'll see what happens,' he answered, regretting the asinine reply.

'Would you like a nose through some of my albums?' asked Paul, lightening the mood.

'Sure, that would be great!'

They spent a few hours drinking more tea, playing tracks Steve hadn't heard since he'd left the States, and smoking some grass. Steve had landed on Paul's Hendrix collection and the temptation was too much.

'You really miss Mike don't you?' said Paul.

It took Steve by surprise, they hadn't discussed it at

all since Steve had told Paul of his friend's death.

'Yeah, a lot.'

'I think he would like it here, he would be at rest here' said Paul. Had he guessed what Steve had been up to? He decided to let it go. Thoy came in, a timely interruption.

'I've made a very light lunch. As it's not too hot yet, I thought perhaps we would eat in the garden.' She thought Paul looked wild, untamed, listening to this farang music. But she knew in an hour or two after lunch he would be cool and organised, ready for his flight.

The garden was a true delight. Paul had a gardener, but Thoy oversaw everything that he did, and together they had created a paradise by the calm waters of the canal. They ate beneath a large parasol, and drank a bottle of Premier Cru Batard-Montrachet. 'My father's favourite wine' said Paul. 'He used to drink it on special occasions, and for me this is a special occasion!'

Paul left for the airport a few hours later, and his absence was keenly felt and immediate. For Steve it posed a question; should he stay or should he go? Thoy was sad, she spent the rest of the early evening arranging flowers carefully picked from the garden.

✳

Paul had some explaining to do. He knew he would have to see Sam in Paris, explain why he was spending so much time in Thailand and try to get Sam to agree to get him off the Phoenix programme. It would be hard, the war was escalating and the government needed all the help it could get. He thought of discussing his meeting with his father's killers, Sam had been a close friend and might understand or, it might flush Sam out – was Paul set up by his own people? In any case, Paul had done the Agency a favour, he had wiped out the dealers who were stealing from them. But it raised a slightly delicate matter of whether the Agency was or wasn't dealing big time in the triangle. Paul thought they were, but did Sam? There was also Sam's relationship with his mother. Were they still lovers? It was their business, but then she might tell Sam about the ring and how Paul had come by it.

He contemplated these questions and others as he lay with his head propped on a Samsonite for a pillow. Three of his co-passengers were regular army, there was a high-ranking marine officer, and someone else from the Agency. Nobody spoke. Despite having lots to think about, the flight as usual was excruciatingly boring and uncomfortable. He wondered why they didn't deck out more C130's with a few seats.

Seventeen hours later the plane touched down on British soil, at a U.S. airbase on the east coast of England. He was driven to Heathrow and took a commercial flight to Paris.

His mother had an elegant apartment on the Isle de Paris, and he arrived there in the morning tired but elated. She had grown older, but she was still beautiful. She greeted him as only a mother can greet her son back from the war. They lunched over another bottle of Batard-Montrachet.

'Pour Papa.' Paul produced the ring. 'It is for you Mamam. I took it from the men who killed Papa, and they are now dead. No-one but you or I must know of this, not Sam, not anyone. You understand?'

His mother was stunned, silent, then she cried. She reached across the table for his hand, squeezed it and whispered, 'It will be our secret!'

Paul ordered a cognac, and they sat quietly together in the restaurant without speaking. They were both thinking of his father. 'I have something else for you back in the apartment Mamam, shall we go?'

In the taxi he asked her about Sam, her life in Paris. She missed home, Vietnam, very much. She kept herself occupied, Sam was often away, she didn't know where, she didn't ask and he didn't say. She had made some friends in Paris, some Vietnamese, some French and some American.

Back in the apartment they reminisced about the old days in Vietnam on the plantation, the servants who had become their friends, the life they led which had gone forever. She had managed to bring some of the antiques which had furnished their house there, and as they sat in the salon, as the afternoon sun felt its way into the elegant building, the sombre fragrance of the teak and mahogany took him back to when he was a little boy. He stood staring up through the palms at the clear blue sky, he heard the splashing of water from the fountain in the garden, it mingled with the scent of the rubber trees and the chatting of the plantation workers.

'Oh, I nearly forgot, excuse me just for one moment.' He left the salon and went to the hallway where he retrieved the Samsonite, removed the false bottom and the seventy-five thousand dollars which lay nestled beneath it. He replaced the bottom, replaced the dollars but this time into the main part of the case and went back into the salon. He opened it in front of his mother. 'This is a present for you. I retrieved it from Papa's killers, it is rightfully yours.' He read her thoughts. 'I'm sure you'll find a use for it. I've given some to the orphans in Saigon, a lot. It's better though if you just keep this between us as, well, you know, it's a lot of money, I think you should put it in a safety deposit box and spend it when you need it, that way you can save your other income.'

'You are a wonderful son! Alright, I won't tell Sam, but when I get a box you'd better have the number just in case. One of my American friends has asked me to go to Virginia with her, I've never been to America Paul, do you think I would like it?'

'Yes, I think you will. It is such a big country, so much to see.'

'Do you think we shall ever go home again my son?'

'I don't know Mamam, we shall have to see. There have been a lot of changes you know, it will take many years, when the war is over perhaps we can go. I don't know, if it becomes a communist country we may not be able to.'

He thought of their old home, of the American chief of staff who was still probably living there, he wondered if it had been mortared or blown up by the V.C.

'Mamam, I have to go, I have some things I must do, and well, you know ...' He walked over to her, put his arms around her and kissed her in the French way on both cheeks. She was tearful, and clutched at him. 'It's all right, I'll be back, very soon.'

Beneath the oppressive heat of the Bangkok suburb where Paul's house nestled, the cool winds of northern Europe began to seem very attractive to Steve. The hours Thoy had spent flower arranging he had spent listening to more Hendrix, finishing off the wine and contemplating. He kept thinking of Kate. 'Your Celtic connection' as Paul had once said. Paul had left him five thousand dollars, 'to tide you over', and the address of the Dutchman in Bangkok. It didn't feel right to stay in the house that night, Thoy would put on a brave face but she was missing Paul and would not find comfort with him, not that night anyway. He went to find her.

She was in the kitchen. 'Ah, I was just going to cook some food for us, you are always hungry!' she smiled.

'Uh, I've gotta go into town. I might not be back for a while.'

If she was a little surprised she didn't show it. She smiled. 'Okay. This time of day it's quicker to go all the way by taxi. Otherwise you would have to wait for the river boat. When you are ready, we can walk and I will show you, you could get a tuk-tuk if you like, they're good fun!'

'Oh I know!' he answered. 'Actually, if its okay with you, I'd sooner go now. I mean …' he felt a little awkward, as if he'd said the wrong thing. Perhaps he should have waited.

'Okay, I'll just lock up and I'll show you the way' she smiled.

They walked along by the canal, the mosquitoes were out and some decent sized rats hopped off the top of an open drain as they walked past. Further along, by the same drain, some children were throwing stones at more rats. It was hot. They walked on in silence until they reached one of the slightly larger streets where tuk-tuks, bicycles, cars, and coaches were driving at various speeds and angles across it.

'Here. You should be able to get a taxi or a tuk-tuk will stop for you. It should cost you about ten baht into town, don't pay more than fifteen' she smiled. He reached forward, put his arms round her waist and drew her towards him. She seemed a little taken back. He kissed her on both cheeks gently, and released her. She was blushing and he realized he had made a mistake.

'Shit, I'm sorry! I forgot.'

'It's okay! She smiled. It's nobody's business but ours. I have learnt one or two things from you as well!' she almost laughed. He almost changed his mind, he almost stayed.

She turned and walked back towards the canal. Thirty seconds later a tuk-tuk screeched to a halt by him and the now familiar bargaining started. He caved in after what seemed like a very long time and agreed to pay twenty baht to the Oriental.

He arrived there about half an hour later, checked in and got the hotel to book him on the next available flight for the U.K. It was nine o'clock in the evening, the flight left at 9 a.m. the following morning.

From the hotel lobby he phoned Paul's connection. They met two hours later in a restaurant overlooking the river. Steve liked the Dutchman, he looked like so many of the people he knew back in California, long blonde hair, blue eyes, tanned. His name was Rudi, and he brought some samples with him. Over noodles, prawns and cold beer they got down to business, and Steve found it a relief not to have to bargain. There were various possible 'deals'. He could take some of the stones for Rudi to Rotterdam, and get paid a direct fee for his trouble. Alternatively he could invest in some of the stones himself, putting up some money and then taking a share of the profit. Or he could simply buy some stones and do what he wanted with them. Rudi was open about his contact, the level of profit and the best ways, in his opinion, of getting them out of Bangkok. This was because he was getting a kick-back from his friend in Rotterdam. He also had a message he wanted Steve to deliver to one of his friends who lived on a barge near the Herengracht.

'He's a nice guy, you'll like him. He grows grass on his barge, it's really good stuff.'

For a second Steve thought of the last time he was in

the Dam, the Orange Julius, Mike.

They agreed that Steve would buy some stones himself and if he wanted to reconvert them at a profit then he could use Rudi's contact and deliver the message, otherwise they would meet up again at some point in the future in Bangkok, hopefully with Paul.

'I don't suppose there's any point in asking where Paul is?' smiled Rudi as he finished his prawns and gulped at his beer.

Steve smiled back. 'I can honestly say I don't know.'

'That sounds like Paul. He once disappeared for six months or so, came back with so many dollars man, I hate to think how he does it!'

Steve got to bed around mid-night. He slept fitfully, despite the air-conditioning and blissful comfort at the Oriental. He got up at around 5 a.m., showered, packed and had breakfast. He'd spent a long time thinking about the stones, and how to conceal them. In the end he decided to simply put them in his pocket along with his loose change. He checked in early enough to get a seat by an exit door, stretched out and resigned himself to the long hours of the flight.

'Been anywhere nice governor?' said the cab driver as they drove west into London from Heathrow. It was raining, Steve looked out over the box-like houses, industrial sheds and the occasional small green field which formed the kind of no mans land between the airport and the suburbs. He followed a raindrop's passage as it splattered on the window and mingled with the others to reach obscurity.

'Nice to be back?' asked the driver.

'I'm American, I'm just visiting here.'

'Oh, I didn't think you got that suntan over here!' said the cabby.

'I guess not' said Steve, hoping to end the conversation.

'Where abouts you from in the States then?' his new found friend persisted.

Steve couldn't lie. 'Mid West.'

'You're a bit of a cowboy then are you?!'

'Guess so' said Steve. It seemed to have done the trick. His friend in front was silent for a while, it lasted long enough to get them to Paddington station. From there he was going to get straight on the next train for the west country.

He had to wait two hours. He was cold, he drank a lot of coffee and ate a cheese sandwich. He had a first class ticket, and had the carriage to himself. He took his shoes off, stretched out across the seat and slept luxuriously for a few hours. He was awakened by the ticket inspector, ten minutes before the train arrived at its destination.

He found a cab outside the station and agreed a thirty pound fare to take him thirty kilometres to the cottage on the moor, nearly fifty dollars! Maybe the tuk-tuks weren't so bad after all. The rain never stopped, it was driven by a strong wind from the Atlantic and slashed at him as he stooped to get into the early 1960's Ford Zephyr. He grasped the nettle. 'Uh, I've been away a while and I'd really like to have the radio on, would you mind?' He was slumped in the back, and made it obvious he was going to go to sleep.

'That's fine by me matey!' He switched the radio on, and David Bowie sang 'Life on Mars'. 'This do you?'

'Couldn't be better!'

That was the sum total of their conversation. Steve had found the perfect cab driver. He stayed awake throughout the journey, pretending to doze, his heart was beating faster with every mile as they approached the old stone cottage. It stood on its own, in a field, and the driver had to stop at the bottom of an unmade track. The lights were on, smoke was trailing across the sky under the wind and rain which tried to force it back down the inglenook below. The wind tore one of the five pound notes from his hand as he paid the cab driver, he scurried after it, stamped on it in the mud and re-presented it.

'That's alright matey, it'll still work alright! Looks like we're building up a storm!'

The front door was unlocked. He opened it quietly, not really knowing why, left his bag by the stairs immediately opposite the door, and tip-toed across the living room through to the kitchen. The door opened back towards him, he pulled it quietly and through the opening he could see Kate, standing towards the sink chopping vegetables. The stove was to her right, and a couple of pots were boiling way, with steam pouring out of one into the kitchen. He crept up behind her, slid his arms around her waist and up over her breasts as he kissed her on the neck. The result was quite dramatic. She twisted and turned, twisted again and came round to face him with a large Japanese vegetable knife in her hand.

'Jesus Mary! You bloody fool, how would I know that was you?! What's the matter with you!?'

'Sorry Katie! Just thought I'd surprise you!' he said a little sheepishly. She looked flushed.

'Well typical now isn't it, you should turn up just when there's some food being cooked! Too much trouble I suppose to phone and let me know you were coming! Sure, I was gonna be going out soon to the restaurant and all, now I'll have to phone them and tell them I'm not going!' Their eyes met, she put the knife down on the cutting board and reached up to put both her arms round his neck, pulling him down towards her. She kissed him hard on the mouth. He started over again, his hands wandering this time up her back, trying to find their way into her blouse. She pushed him off, laughing. 'I see you're as patient as ever! There's a bottle of wine in the fridge, why don't you open that now and have some of this food. Are you hungry?' She answered it for herself. 'Silly question!'

'I've got something for you Babes!' He felt in the side of his bag, pulled out a piece of Thai silk, which covered a Burmese lacquered box. Inside was a large emerald he'd bought from Rudi.

'Why it's beautiful! Emerald isn't it? She couldn't

help herself, she continued. 'I hate to think where you got it from!'

'It's okay. I made a few bucks and spent them on you. Nothing wrong with that is there?!'

'No, nothing at all!' she laughed. She pulled him towards her again, and this time, when his hands were searching inside her blouse, they found what they were looking for.

It was a wild night, the wind and rain hammered against the windows, the trees bent beneath the force of the storm. They lay in front of the fire, in a secret world that only they could share. In the early hours of the morning the storm abated, the wind cleared the sky and the moon and stars appeared behind heavy silver clouds. They looked out across the fields, two deer had ventured from the woodland close by and a fox ran the length of the field before turning and darting into the undergrowth at the edge of the treeline. They made love again.

In the morning Kate left Steve sleeping, and walked across the fields beneath the chorus of the woodland birds. A blackbird set the alarm, rabbits in the distance scurried back into their holes along the banks, woodpigeons left the high trees in small flocks, a dog barked on the farm nearby. She walked back slowly to the cottage as the sun rose and set the hills on fire in the distance. Steve had woken up and was eating a banana he had found in the kitchen.

'Suits you!' laughed Kate. 'The milkman will be here in a minute!' she warned.

'I don't think there's any bananas left!' he countered. 'What are you up to today, are you going into the restaurant?'

'No. I'm all yours' she giggled. 'Let them eat bananas!'

He smiled and caught hold of her again in his arms. 'There's just one thing I want to do before I can really relax. It's that prayer book, you know, from Father Wallace. I think I should return it to him. It's been on my mind. Do you feel like a walk over there with me sometime today?'

'I do. But I was lying about the milk, actually I get it from the farm up the road now, take this jug up there and they fill it up for me free. It's fantastic, and the cat loves it! I need to do that and there's no food in the house'. Steve looked up. 'Maybe I should get all that together and you could wander over and see the priest yourself. I'm sure you'd prefer to do that anyway wouldn't you?'

'Well, if I get there early I could probably catch him in and then you'd have done the milk and everything and we could meet up back here?'

'Carry on where we left off?!' laughed Kate.

The sun was out in full strength and Steve walked up the narrow cobbled street to Father Wallace's terraced house. Rain from the night before was trapped in large puddles, they shimmered in the stillness like glass and reflected the row of cottages above them. He held the leather-bound prayer book in his hand, and knocked on the priest's door. It creaked open, and the benign but astute face of the priest appeared. 'Ah well now! If it's not my young American friend! How are you? Won't you come in!' He ushered Steve into the living room, where the bookcase and log fire took him back to the dark night before he left.

'I've brought you this back, Father' said Steve, coming straight to the point.

'Ah well now, that's nice! I hope it was useful?' said the priest raising his voice at the end.

'Yes, yes it was. I took your advice and did a bit of travelling. I ended up in Thailand and spent a little bit of time in a monastery there and told the monks the story about my friend. They were understanding and they said some prayers for him too. I feel much better about it all now.'

'Ah, well now. That's alright then. I did one or two little things of my own, so hopefully between us he'll be feeling alright now. I don't think you should worry anymore. Looks to me like you're not anyway! Now tell me, how's that fine young Irish girl of yours? Father Wallace looked at Steve knowingly.

Beneath his suntan Steve blushed. 'She's fine Father thank you' then adding 'as I'm sure you know fine well!'

The Father laughed. 'Well I see she's been teaching you to speak properly anyway! I was just about to have a wee drop of this, have you got time?' His hand rested on a bottle of whisky.

'Yes, that would be great, thank you!'

Father Wallace poured out two good measures.

'Um, very nice! Bushmills. Last one you had was from Scotland.'

Steve honestly couldn't tell the difference, and said as much.

'Ah well now, that will give you an excuse to come and see me again, you need to be able to tell the difference, an educated young fella like you!' The priest was delighted.

They finished the drink and Steve made ready to go.

'Now you tell young Kate and her friend Sarah I'd like to see them once in a while – they're welcome anytime!' He laughed. They shook hands and Steve felt the priest could have crushed him with one blow, he could feel the strength in the hand.

Walking back down the narrow street, he thought of Paul. He still had some explaining to do to Kate. Where was Paul now? For all he knew he could be close by, he'd said Paris but that could have meant anything. He could turn up anytime, and the worrying thing was, Steve wanted him to.

He knew this was just the beginning.